I set everything out on the kitchen table and said the spell. "Powers that be, harken to me. Send me success in the thing I confess. To the universe proffering, I make this offering. I want to be Juliet. Please, please, please, please, please. Make me Juliet."

And I lit the match.

There was a quiet whoosh and orange flames licked up all over my little volcano. The red cube burned. It was pretty. Very theatrical.

But it was casting too much light. And for some reason, the light was coming from over my head.

I jerked my head up and saw a bright white glow hanging about three feet over the table, right over my flame.

"Aaah?" I said. Or something like that.

And with the bright light came a sound like a low bass note that turned into a sort of rumbling thrill, something like an earthquake.

Everyone in California knows what you're supposed to do when a quake hits. You stand in a doorway. And that's what I did, even though this was no quake and I knew it. I clutched the door frame with both hands while the white light suddenly filled the whole kitchen, so bright I couldn't see anything. There was a bang, and the light was gone.

My baking dish was shattered. It lay in two exact halves on the floor. Smoke curled up from each one of them, but there was no crust. They were clean as a pair of very clean whistles.

But that was not the main thing I noticed. No, the main thing I noticed was the tall young man standing on the table in the middle of my glass round. He was about my age, and for some reason he was dressed in tights and boots and a big poofy shirt like he was supposed to be in a play like, say, *Romeo and Juliet*.

He even looked a little like Shakespeare.

Long hair, a bit of a beard…

I screamed.

Also by Douglas Rees
from Harlequin TEEN

Majix: Notes from a Serious Teen Witch

The Juliet Spell

Douglas Rees

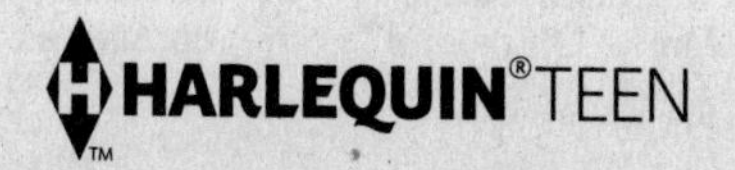

ISBN-13: 978-0-373-21039-8

THE JULIET SPELL

This edition published by arrangement with Harlequin Books S.A.

For questions and comments about the quality of this book please contact us at Customer_eCare@Harlequin.ca.

www.HarlequinTEEN.com

Printed in U.S.A.

To Carol Wolf

Chapter One

"Miranda Hoberman."

That was me. My turn. My chance. My audition. Now. With all the cool I could muster, which felt like exactly none, I left my seat and climbed up onto the stage.

Down in the front row, Mr. Gillinger glared at me, looked at my audition sheet and glared at me again.

"*You're* reading for Juliet?" he drawled in his deep voice.

"Yes," I gulped.

"Very well, go ahead."

Bobby Ruspoli grinned, sizing me up. He was already Romeo, and everyone knew it. It just hadn't been announced, yet. Mr. Gillinger would post his name along with the rest of the cast on the theater office door tomorrow or the next day. But we all knew he was Romeo before the play was ever announced, the way people in drama know who's going to get what, when the fix is in. So with that weight off his mind, handsome Bobby was checking out every girl who might be his Juliet.

As if I wasn't nervous enough. As if I hadn't been studying this part every day since it had been announced that we were doing *Romeo and Juliet.* As if I hadn't spent the last week lying awake nights worrying and thinking about how to do this moment better, I had to have Bobby checking out my boobs and butt. As if—

"Begin," Mr. Gillinger commanded.

Bobby shrugged, inhaled, the way he'd seen real actors do in some of the acting DVDs we'd watched in class, and announced:

"He jests at scars that never felt a wound."

Then he looked up, like I was hanging from one of the Fresnel lamps that were glaring down on us, instead of standing right in front of him, shaking.

"But soft! What light is this that through yonder window breaks?
It is the east, and Juliet is the sun.
Arise, fair sun, and kill the envious moon,
Who is already sick and pale with grief
That thou her maid art far more fair than she. . . ."

He rattled off the next nineteen lines of the speech exactly the way he had done them all afternoon, racing down to:

"O that I were a glove upon thy hand, that I might touch that cheek."

My turn. My line: "Ay me!"

I know, it sounds lame. But I said it like I wanted to die. Because that's how Juliet feels right then. But had it been too much?

Bobby went on, "She speaks."

Out in the auditorium, someone giggled.

Bobby continued.

"Oh, speak again, bright angel, for thou art
As glorious to this night, being o'er my head,
As is a winged messenger of heaven
Unto the white upturned wond'ring eyes
Of mortals that fall back to gaze on him,
When he bestrides the lazy-pacing clouds
And sails upon the bosom of the air."

Me again. My first real line in the scene. The one everybody knows—usually wrong: "O Romeo, Romeo! Wherefore art thou Romeo?"

You probably thought Juliet was asking where Romeo is, right? Wrong. She has no idea he's anywhere around. He's just been thrown out of the party her father was giving. He's gone. She's asking why the guy's name has to be Romeo, and the next lines make that clear.

"Deny thy father and refuse thy name;
Or, if thou wilt not, be but sworn my love,
And I'll no longer be a Capulet."

"Shall I hear more, or shall I speak at this?" Bobby asked the invisible balcony where Juliet was supposed to be standing.

Me:

"'Tis but thy name that is my enemy;
Thou art thyself, though not a Montague.
What's a Montague?—"

"Thank you," Mr. Gillinger said. Like he was saying "Thank you for shutting up now, please."

"Auh?" I said. I was kind of surprised. That was an awfully short audition.

"Let's see. Next. Vivian Brandstedt. Also Juliet, right?" Mr. Gillinger said.

I got down off the stage. I was done. I could leave. But I wanted to see what the rest of my competition looked like.

I went to the far back of the auditorium and moved into a corner seat.

Vivian Brandstedt slithered up onstage and began to play Juliet like she'd been the hottest babe in Verona. It was funny, except that Vivian really was a hot babe, so nobody thought it was funny but me. Certainly Bobby didn't. He fluffed his lines twice. Of course, it was hard for him to talk with his tongue hanging out of his mouth like that.

Mr. Gillinger let Vivian go on all the way to the end of the scene. He even read the nurse's offstage lines to keep the thing going to the point where Juliet says,

"Good night, good night. Parting is such sweet sorrow
That I shall say good night till it be morrow."

And Vivian wasn't bad. She just read it like she was tossing Romeo down her panties and her room key.

Why, why, why hadn't Mr. Gillinger let me read the whole scene? Was I that bad, or was I so good that he didn't need to see any more of me? Or was Juliet pre-cast like Romeo?

There was a noise down at the end of the row and a shape came toward me. Drew Jenkins.

He sat down beside me and whispered, "You were good. You get it."

Then he got up and went back down to the front row where he'd been.

I was absurdly grateful. Drew Jenkins, for reasons nobody could understand, was total BF best friends with Bobby Ruspoli, and if Drew liked me, maybe Bobby did, too. And maybe Bobby would say so to Mr. Gillinger and maybe—or maybe Drew had inside information. Maybe "You get it" meant "I just saw Gillinger's notes. You've got the part," not just "You get who Juliet is in this scene." Or maybe Drew had some kind of weird hold over Mr. Gillinger and was going to make him cast me—Drew was kind of mysterious for a sixteen-year-old geek. He knew all kinds of things. Maybe he had something on Gillinger, like an old arrest for marrying his own ego.

I forced myself to stop thinking like that. I didn't want the part because Bobby Ruspoli liked me, or even because Mr. Gillinger did (which would be amazing, since Mr. Gillinger thought he should be directing on Broadway and didn't like anybody). I wanted to play Juliet because I was the best actor who read for it, not because some guy hanging out with some guy thought I was good.

Which is not to say I wouldn't have taken the part under any conditions. Play Juliet in Swahili? I'll learn it.

But if I wasn't going to think about whether Drew's opinion counted with Bobby and Bobby's opinion counted with Mr. Gillinger, or whatever, what was I going to think about? I was going to think about why I hadn't been allowed to finish the scene. Of course.

Had I said "Ay me," too loudly, or not loudly enough? Had I sounded convincing when I said "Wherefore art thou Romeo?" Did I even sound like I knew what it meant? Yes, I had. No, I hadn't. Yes, I—

He likes me, he likes me not. He likes me, he likes me not. That was what it came down to, and I couldn't stop obsessing even though I knew it was all out of my hands.

Two more girls read for Juliet that afternoon. They were both awful. I'm not just saying that. They were awful. One read like she was reciting a recipe: "Take one part Romeo and one part Juliet and stir until done. Then separate and—"

And the other was total emo.

"O Romeo, Romeo WHY ART THOU CALLED ROMEO?"

(Which is not the line, right?)

"DENY thy father and REFUSE thy NAME;
Or if thou wilt NOT, be but sworn my LOVE,
And I'll no LONGER BE A CAPULET."

When she was done, and the stage was awash in her saliva, Mr. Gillinger stood up. He looked over the fifty or so of us sitting there, people from his drama classes, people from outside the high school who'd come down to read in the middle of the day—a half-hundred theater junkies, hanging on his every word.

He seemed to be enjoying it. I always thought this moment, when his opinion was the only thing that counted to a roomful of people, was the real reason Gillinger had decided to teach drama. Or maybe it was just the only reason he had left, after so many years of doing it. Anyway, I'd been watching him direct for a couple of years now and something about the set of his once-handsome head always said "God, I'm good." He didn't even need to open his mouth to be arrogant.

Gillinger sighed. "I'm not seeing what I want here. I'm not seeing what I need to see at all. Some of you know I didn't want to do this play. It was forced on me by the administration when they wouldn't approve my plans to produce *The Tragical History of Doctor Faustus* with the nude scenes. They said they'd permit the production only if everyone stayed fully clothed. I said the play had been successfully produced with the roles of Helen of Troy, and the Devil Woman, unclothed any number of times since the 1960s. They said there were children—meaning you high-school students—involved in the play. I said that I had no intention of casting Helen as anything but what she was, a woman of twenty-three to thirty-three. And as for the Devil Woman, she could be any age. She is, after all, a demon. Demons are ageless.

"They said that didn't matter, everyone would have to stay dressed. I asked if they really thought that the children to whom they alluded had never seen a naked human body, when they could call up images involving every possible configuration of lust on the electronic goodies that they carried in their pockets, and study them. They said that didn't matter, either, as long as they didn't do it on school grounds. I said I wouldn't do the play any other way. They said, in that case, I would have to do something else, and I said, in that case, you'll have to decide what it is. Right now. What play, in your vast wisdom and deep knowledge of classical theater will you permit to be staged at this school? They said the first thing that came into their heads, and that thing was *Romeo and Juliet,* William Shakespeare's most overrated piece of hackwork. Probably, it is the only work of Shakespeare's that they have ever heard of."

Gillinger sighed again and closed his eyes. "The point is, if I am going to do this show at all, I am going to do it right. I will not, repeat, not, be satisfied with anything less than an outstanding production. And that, unfortunately, will require at least some outstanding actors. Now, I've seen a few of you who are—good. I've seen a few more who aren't bad. And many of you will do for the servants. This play is, after all, servant central. But there are key roles that cannot be filled by anyone I've seen so far.

"Fortunately, since this production is being funded by a grant from the city, it is, as you all know, open to the community at large. Thus, I do not have to cast just from the shallow talent pool at dear old Steinbeck High. So I'm doing something I'd rather not do, but which the lack of talent in this entire community is forcing on me. I am, in desperation, extending tryouts one more day. Go home, tell your friends if they have any acting ability at all to get down here and save this show. Otherwise—" He shrugged.

Maybe that meant "Otherwise I will not direct anything, and take the consequences." Maybe it didn't mean anything. Gillinger strode off into the wings with his jacket trailing from his shoulders like a cape.

That was it. We were done here. All over the theater there were thumping sounds as the seats went up and people started for the doors.

I slung my backpack and slid down the row to the aisle.

Bobby and Drew passed me.

"Break it," Bobby said with a grin and a nod in my direction. This was Bobby's version of "break a leg," which is what theater types wish each other for luck before a show, which this wasn't. But Bobby said "break it" any time. He thought it made him sound like a professional.

Drew gave me a thumbs-up, then flashed two fingers side by side.

What was that supposed to mean?

All the way home I wondered about that.

If it didn't mean some weird sex thing, which was virtually unthinkable given how straight-edge Drew seemed to be, it probably was supposed to mean, "I think you're the best one. But it's between you and one other."

Food for thought. Or, actually, dessert for obsession. If I was one, who was the other? Vivian the Terminally Hot? Or was it somebody who'd read the day before, when I couldn't come to tryouts? Who would that have been? Were they even in our school?

Blah, blah, blah. I wished, in a brief rational moment, that I had a different head with something else in it. But we are all stuck with the heads we have, and mine was trying to think of anything I could do that I hadn't already done to get that part.

This was not entirely and completely because I was a total drama nerd who only cared about getting a lead. That was a lot of it—but I had a reason all my own that nobody else did.

My mother had never played Juliet.

Right now you're thinking, "So what? My mother never played Juliet. Nobody's mother I know ever played Juliet. And none of the mothers' mothers ever played Juliet. Your mother is right on track." Which would be true, except that, before she was a nurse, my mother was an actor.

You never heard of her. Which means she was just like ninety-nine and nine-tenths percent of all the actors in America. But she went to Juilliard, and when she graduated she came out to the West Coast and joined what they call The I-5 Repertory Company.

The I-5 is the freeway that runs between Seattle and San Diego, and there are actors who make their living—or almost make a living—moving up and down it. There's a lot of theater in Seattle, some in Portland, and there's the Shakespeare Festival in Ashland, Oregon, which is huge. There's work in San Francisco and Sacramento and Los Angeles and San Diego if you can get it, and there are side trips to places like Austin.

That's what my mother did for eight years. She was good, she was pretty and twice she was nearly cast as Juliet, once in Ashland and once in San Diego.

When she turned thirty and she was still just almost making a living, and she gave up acting and went into a nursing program, the one regret she had was that she'd never played that part.

She'd plowed though nursing school, which she loved, gotten out and found work right away at Bannerman Hospital here in Guadalupe, California, met my dad and had me. And I'd caught the acting bug from her, and we'd all been happier than most people I knew, until my dad, who had a Ph.D. in psychology, decided he needed to "develop as an individual" and told Mom he was taking off.

I hadn't seen him since ninth grade. That was almost two years. As far as we knew, he was wandering around America, sometimes working, sometimes not. Once in a while, we got a postcard.

Mom and I kept hoping he'd come back.

If I could play Juliet, I would give my performance to my mom. I would put it in the program as a dedication and say something nice. In one way, it wouldn't be much. But in another way, it would be gigantic. It would be a way of saying "I love you" in big, fat, Elizabethan letters.

When I got home, the house was quiet. No surprise there. Mom was working a double shift over at Bannerman and wasn't supposed to be home until tomorrow morning. But the note on the bulletin board where we communicated with each other *was* surprising:

CHILD SUPPORT! Your dad paid up. That means this is my last double shift at the hospital for a while. I'll be home tomorrow about seven-thirty. Who knows? I might even see you before you go to school. It'd be nice to touch base with you again before you graduate.
Love,
Mom

My parents weren't divorced. If they'd been divorced, things might actually have been better for us. Then at least we'd have had the law on our side when Dad didn't pay the money he'd promised to help keep me alive. But they were just "separated." He paid when he paid. Which was somewhere between not often and never. And when he did pay, it wasn't much. But today there was a check on the fridge, and it was big. Almost a whole year's back cash for the privilege of not seeing me.

I tried to ignore the pang that gave me, and thought about the good things that the money would mean. A dinner out with Mom to celebrate was one thing for sure. And some new school clothes. And some bills paid off. And Mom working eight hours a day instead of sixteen, at least for a while. Thank you, Daddy, wherever you are. For a few minutes, I wasn't thinking about playing/not playing Juliet.

But then I was again.

The child support was a sign. When you're an actor, everything is a sign of something else. Actors are the most superstitious people on the planet. And it was obviously a good sign. Anything I did now to move things in my direction would work. That's what I told myself.

And it made me think of something else. A whole new obsession. Maybe, if I played Juliet, my dad would come home. I mean, I'd tried out, and here was the child support. Therefore, if I got the part, he'd come back. Perfectly logical.

This is what shrinks like Dad call fantasizing. They will tell you that it is immature and a sign of emotional distress. They will also tell you that it doesn't work.

But I had nothing to lose by believing it. And fantasy is only fantasy *if* it doesn't work. So I went into my room and got out my spell kit.

I'd read about spell kits the year before in a book called *Spellcraft For the Average Teen.* The writer, who called herself Aurora Skye, had written a sort-of cookbook for how to get things you wanted. And I'd put mine together and started using it daily.

What did I want? I wanted my father to come home. And I'd cast spells for it for over a month, every afternoon when Mom wasn't home, which was pretty much all of them. They were called drawing spells, because they were supposed to draw the person to you.

You do not need me to tell you how well they worked. Daddy was still out there somewhere. But now was different. There was that check. That big check that meant he'd remembered us. Remembered me. So, fantasizing said, it was time. Aurora Skye said it, too. If a spell didn't work, she wrote over and over again, don't give up. Keep casting and the spell will work in its own time. Today, right now, I believed it.

So I got out the cardboard box where I kept the odds and ends you needed to cast spells and flipped open the book to Spells For Success. The chapter had a lot of subheadings: Success in Love, Success in Sports, Success on Tests, but nothing that specifically said Success in Getting Cast as Juliet. The closest I could come was Success in Becoming Famous.

First, draw a perfect circle eighteen inches across. (Everyone who's taken geometry for a day knows there's no such thing in real life as a perfect circle. This is probably the second-best escape clause anybody ever had for when something magical doesn't work. The best is, "It must not be time." But what I had for a circle was a round eighteen-inch piece of glass, a little tabletop I'd gotten at the garden section of a hardware store. It was better than anything I could have drawn.)

Next, mix ½ cup Epsom salts and ¼ cup rubbing alcohol in a baking dish. Form into a volcano shape. (This was pretty much the equivalent of bake at 350 degrees, apparently. Most of the spells started this way.)

Place in the cone of the volcano one cube of sugar dyed red. (I had a few left over from last year. They were faded to a sort of brown now, but I wasn't in a mood to be fussy. They'd been red once.)

Place the dish in the exact center of the circle. (Ah, yes. There's that word again. Exact. I lined it up with a ruler on four sides. But how could anything ever be exactly exact?)

Say the following spell: "Powers that be, harken to me. Send me success in the thing I confess. To the universe proffering, I make this offering." Then say what it is that you want.

Light the volcano with an ordinary wooden match that has been blessed by a Practitioner. (A Practitioner is what the book calls people who sell stuff for spells. I had a box of Practitioner Matches with three left in it.)

When the alcohol is consumed, a thick crust will be left in the bottom of the dish. The crust is the obstacles in your path burned away. When the dish has cooled, remove this reverently to the trash.

I set everything out on the kitchen table and said the spell. "Powers that be, harken to me. Send me success in the thing I confess. To the universe proffering, I make this offering. I want to be Juliet. Please, please, please, please, please. Make me Juliet."

And I lit the match.

There was a quiet whoosh and orange flames licked up all over my little volcano. The red cube burned. It was pretty. Very theatrical.

But it was casting too much light. And for some reason, the light was coming from over my head, like a stage light.

I jerked my head up and saw a bright white glow hanging about three feet over the table, right over my flame.

"Aaah?" I said. Or maybe Uuuuuh? Anyway it was something like that.

And with the bright light came a sound like a low bass note that turned into a sort of rumbling thrill, something like an earthquake.

Everyone in California knows what you're supposed to do when a quake hits. You stand in a doorway. And that's what I did, even though this was no quake and I knew it. I clutched the door frame with both hands while the white light suddenly filled the whole kitchen, so bright I couldn't see anything. There was a bang, and the light was gone.

My baking dish was shattered. It lay in two exact halves

on the floor. Smoke curled up from each one of them, but there was no crust. They were clean as a pair of very clean whistles.

But that was not the main thing I noticed. No, the main thing I noticed was the tall young man standing on the table in the middle of my glass round. He was about my age, and for some reason he was dressed in tights and boots and a big poofy shirt like he was supposed to be in a play like, say, *Romeo and Juliet*.

He even looked a little like Shakespeare.

Long hair, a bit of a beard…

I screamed.

He smiled, held up one hand, got down on one knee, bowed his head to me and said some words in a language I didn't understand.

"Speak English," I said.

The boy looked up, shocked. "Ye're never Helen of Troy," the boy said, and leapt to his feet.

"What?" I said.

"These are never the topless towers of Illium," the boy said, looking around the kitchen wildly.

I screamed again, and he, for some reason, crossed himself, yanked a crucifix out from under his shirt, held it out at me like he thought it was a shield, and shouted, "Doctor D., Doctor D., where are ye?"

Chapter Two

After those frantic moments, we just stared at each other for a bit.

Finally, the boy gulped. I could see his cross was trembling in his hand. He wasn't the only one trembling.

"What ha' ye done wi' Doctor D.?"

"Who the hell are you?" I said.

"Who in hell are *ye?*" he asked.

"What are you doing here? How did you do that? What do you want?" I shrieked.

I'd cast a spell and it had worked. But it hadn't worked right. Something was very, very wrong, and I didn't have a clue what it was, or how to fix it. I was scared, more scared than I'd known I could be.

"Damned spirit, I charge thee, make Doctor D. appear!" the boy shouted. "By the power of the Cross I command thee!"

That made me mad. It was like some guy coming to your door trying to sell you his religion. And being scared already, being mad on top of it made me furious.

"Who the hell are you?" I said again. "What did you just do?"

"I am friend and follower to Doctor D.," he said. "Who has power over such as ye. Ye know better than I how I come to be here. Release me and return me to him."

"Get out of here," I said. "Go back where you came from."

"Summon Doctor D., or send me back," the boy said. "I'll not leave this circle."

"Shut up and get off the table," I said, and my voice was so tough even I was scared of it. "Get off right now. It wobbles."

"Ha, ha. Ye'd like that very well," the boy sneered. "Ye know well ye cannot hurt me so long as I remain within me circle."

"It's my circle," I said.

"It is?" He looked down, and saw my round tabletop. "Oh, God, I am truly lost. Saint Mary, help me now."

"If you don't shut up and get off my table and get out of here, I'm calling 911," I said, pulling out my cell phone.

He cringed when he saw it.

"No hellish engine shall conjure me from this spot," he said. "Fetch ye Doctor D. at once, devil thing." He waved his cross around some more.

I punched in 911.

"All of our lines are busy now," a so-friendly recording told me. "Please wait and your call will be answered in the order in which it was received."

"Shit," I said.

"Doctor D.! Doctor D.!" the boy shouted. "Come ye to me."

"The cops are coming," I said, waving my cell phone. "I just said 'shit' because I'm excited."

"Doctor D.!"

Then I had a wild idea. Before Dad went off to develop himself, he used to work out of the house. Maybe this guy was some new kind of crazy, and had come looking for him. This wouldn't explain little things, like how he got here out of thin air, but like I said, it was a wild idea.

"Are you looking for my dad?" I said. "He's a doctor, but he's gone. He left us. But nobody calls him Doctor D."

"Nay, ye evil wight, I call on Doctor John Dee—John Dee, the greatest man in England. What have ye done with him?"

I held the phone to my ear.

"—your call will be answered—"

A weird cold calm came over me. Whatever was going on, this guy was more frightened of it than I was. I could take control of this situation if I could get control of myself. Treat him like Dad would have: like a patient. Even if he wasn't crazy, the situation was.

"If you get down off the table and sit down at it and calm down a little, I'll put the phone away and try to help you," I said. "Otherwise, you can explain it to the cops when they get here."

"If ye are not a demon, give me a sign," the boy said.

"What kind of a sign do you want?"

"Ye must say the Lord's Prayer."

"I'm not going to pray," I said.

"Aha! I knew ye were a servant of the evil one! Help me, Doctor Dee, help me!"

"Oh, all right, damn it. One line. Okay?" I tried to remember Sunday school, but I'd only gone about six times and I hadn't really liked it. Then I recalled something… "'Our Father who art in heaven.' Now get the fuck down."

The boy looked really confused now. "Ye said the words," he said. "Ye said the words and did not burst into flames."

"Yessss... Now get down. And sit down over there."

"If ye are not a demon, are ye an angel?" the boy asked.

"No," I said. "Get down."

"Then are ye a fairy?"

"Not even close. Get down. That table really does have a weak leg. I'm not kidding."

"Return Doctor Dee and I will," the boy said.

"I don't know where he is," I replied. "You're the only one here besides me, and you shouldn't be. But if you'll start calming down I'll try to help you."

"Tell me first what manner of creature ye be. Tell me truly by the power of the Cross."

"I'm just a girl who doesn't like people breaking into her house and pitching their religion at her," I said. "Especially when they erupt out of thin air."

"A girl? Nay, wench. Ye are like no girl on earth. Ye dress in pants like a Tartary savage, ye'er arms are bare as sticks. Ye'er hair is shorter than mine own. Ye speak strange words in an unknown accent. And ye've a—a conjuring thing there in ye'er hand to summon— Copse, ye'er familiar, I doubt not. Tell me what ye truly are."

"This isn't getting us anywhere," I said, trying for calm again. "Why don't you get down off the table and sit over there in the corner and tell me what you think is going on? 'Cause I don't have a clue."

"I'll not—ye are Queen Mab, or one of her servants."

Mab, I thought. *Queen of the fairies. Mercutio talks about her in* Romeo and Juliet. *He thinks I'm her?*

Then the table collapsed. The boy fell backwards, my little round tabletop flew out from under his feet, and his head hit the wall.

"Ow! Blessed Saint Mary, save me now," he yelped.

"Damn it, I told you that leg was weak," I said.

"Don't turn me into anything," the boy begged. "I implore you, spirit, or fairy, or whatever thing ye be, have mercy on a poor lost soul."

I put the cell phone to my ear again.

"—in the order it was received—"

The boy was cowering in the corner now.

"In the name of the Father, the Son, and the Holy Ghost, amen," he said, crossing himself a couple of times.

Well, at least I had him off the table and into the corner.

"Sit. Stay," I commanded, like he was a dog, and pointed the phone at him.

He whimpered and drew his knees up to his chest.

One of the things Dad always said about dealing with crazy people was that, before you could help them, you had to find out what reality they were living in.

"Okay," I said. "I'll have mercy on you, I promise."

"Swear you will not turn me into a toad or other loathsome creature," the boy said.

"I swear not to turn you into anything. Now, my name's Miranda. What's yours?"

"Edmund's me name."

"Fine," I said. "Now, where are you from, Edmund? And how did you get here?" My voice was getting calmer. Almost like Dad's shrink voice. He would have been proud of me.

"London," he said. "Though as ye can tell from me accent I'm not born there."

"Actually, I wouldn't have known that," I said. "Where are you from originally?"

"Warwickshire, of course."

"Okay. And who's this Doctor Dee?"

"As I told ye, Doctor John Dee is the greatest man in England. A mighty mind that knows everything, a valiant heart that dares everything, even the darkest depths of knowledge. Cousin of the queen, friend of all the greats of England. Ye must know of him!"

"Nope. Never heard of him," I said, kind of amazed he expected me to know some guy half-across the world. "But go on. Tell me what he has to do with you."

"We were in his secret rooms in Cheapside.... Doctor Dee was casting a spell. A necromancy." He crossed himself again. "Greatly have we offended. Thus am I punished. Oh, my God, have mercy."

"Just get back to your story," I said slowly and calmly. "What's a necro—what you said?"

"We meant to raise the ghost of Helen of Troy," he said. "For Doctor Dee, necromancy remains the last great thing undone. He wished to question her about the *Iliad.* To know how truly it depicted the battles. For me—fool that I am, I wanted to see Helen. To see 'the face that launched a thousand ships and burned the topless towers of Ilium.' 'Twas why I addressed ye in Greek at first."

I was actually calming down a little. And because I was, my legs started shaking really bad. "Edmund, I'm going to sit down now. Don't be afraid."

He didn't say anything.

I sat down beside the broken table. That felt better.

There's a quick test they give you to find out if you're crazy or not. If you're ever taken to the hospital unconscious they'll give it to you when you wake up. Here it goes.

"Edmund, I'm going to ask you five questions. Real easy ones, okay?"

"What means 'okay'?"

"Okay? It doesn't mean anything. I mean, it means a lot of things. It just means okay, okay?"

"I'll not answer any more questions of yours, save you answer as many questions of mine," he said.

"Okay," I said. "In this case, that means 'yes.' Okay?"

"Yes. Okay."

"First question. What's your name?"

"Edmund Shakeshaft," he said.

"Almost like the writer."

"Writer?" he said, as if he didn't know the word.

"Never mind. You're Edmund Shakeshaft. Fine. Second question. What country is this?"

"I've never a notion," Edmund said. "What country is this?"

I decided to tell him. "The United States of America."

"The *what* of America?"

"Let's go on," I said. "You can ask your questions next. Third question. What year is this?"

"1597."

"Fourth question. What day is this?"

"'Tis the Ides of March," he said.

"Which is what day of what month?" I said.

"'Tis March the fifteent', o'course, or a day on either side."

Maybe it was the Ides of March where he'd been, but here it was the beginning of May.

"One more question," I said, knowing it would make no sense to him. "Who's the president of the United States?"

"Who is the what of the what?"

"That's good, Edmund. We're done. Now you get five questions."

Edmund shifted a little. He was getting a bit more comfortable, too.

"First question. Tell me what ye truly are."

"I already did. I'm a girl named Miranda Hoberman. I'm

not a fairy, or a demon, or any of the other things you think I might be. I'm a human being just like you."

"'Tis easier to believe ye are a fairy.... But ye said a bit of the Lord's Prayer, which they say no unhallowed wight could do. So I suppose I must believe ye. Well, me next question is, if this be the Americas, what part of them am I in?"

"California," I said. "It's part of the United States."

"Nay, 'tis part of the Viceroyalty of New Spain," he said. "Nueva España. Doctor Dee has shown me maps. Why d'ye not speak Spanish?"

"I'll try to explain later," I said. "Go on."

"What year is it?"

When I told him, he turned pale. "How can it be? I'm never four hundred years and more in the future."

"It's the twenty-first century," I said.

Edmund was quiet for a long string of minutes. Then he said. "Everyone's dead. All me friends, all me family. Doctor Dee and everyone. Even the queen must be dead by now, and we thought she'd never die." He looked so shocked I felt sorry for him. And, I realized right then that I believed him. I had to. Nothing else made any sense.

I held my phone to my ear.

"—order in which—"

I switched it off and stuffed it in my pocket. Being lost in time while Elizabethan wasn't a crime in California.

"I have just one more question," Edmund said. "'Tis a boon I would beg of ye. Will ye help me back. Back to me own time?"

"Edmund," I said. "I'm sorry. I don't know how this happened. I don't know if it's something Doctor Dee did, or something I did, or something that just fell on you out of nowhere. I don't know how to reverse it. But I will help you all I can. And so will my mother when she gets home. Okay?"

Edmund began to cry.

Chapter Three

Edmund's shoulders shook. His breath came in terrible gasps. He cried out to God, Saint Mary Mother of God, and Jesus. He called to his mother, his father, to Doctor Dee, and a lot of other names. Then he just wept. I'd never seen a man cry like that. I'd never seen anybody cry like that except my mother when my father left.

I felt so sorry for him. Strange as this whole thing was for me, at least I was still in my own time, with everything I knew about still around me. My mom and I had lost my dad. But Edmund had lost a whole world. And there was no way to get it back. I just sat with my hands in my lap wishing I could think of anything that would help.

Finally, when he had cried himself out, he crossed himself and said, "I am an Englishman. Many of us have been cast on strange strands before this. Come what may, I am still Edmund Shakeshaft. I thank ye, Miranda Hoberman. May God reward your kindness to me."

"You're welcome, Edmund," I said. And then suddenly I had a brilliant idea. "Would you like some tea?"

"Tea?" he said, in a voice that was still shaking.

"Yeah. Mom and I have lots of different kinds."

"What is tea?" he asked.

"I thought all you English guys drank tea all the time," I said.

"No," Edmund said. "Never heard of tea."

"Well, I'd like some," I said, hoping it was just a language thing. "Let me make a cup."

I got up and went over to the stove. I shook the kettle, heard that there was no water in it, and filled it from the tap.

"How does yon work?" he said.

"I don't really know," I said. "Water pressure, I guess."

I went back to the stove and turned on one of the burners.

Edmund stood up to get a better look. Dad would have thought that was a good sign. Getting interested in his surroundings.

"How is't ye can cook without fire?" he said as the burner began to glow.

"It's electric," I said. "Sort of like lightning, but not dangerous. Look." I walked over to the light switch and flicked it. The light over the table came on.

Edmund stared up at the ceiling. He didn't look happy.

"Don't panic," I quickly said. "It's not black magic or anything like that. It's just science. Everybody does this. You can do it."

"I can?"

I turned off the light. "Come on," I said. "First lesson in twenty-first-century living."

He slid along the wall until he was standing beside the light switch.

"Since this is me first time, must I say any special words?" he asked me.

"No. Just push up on the switch."

He did, and the light, of course, came on. He turned it off. He turned it on. He did it back and forth until the teakettle whistled.

"See if you can prop up the table and we'll sit down," I said.

While Edmund crawled under the table and tried to stick the leg back on, I got out two mugs and filled them with hot water and tea bags. I figured English breakfast blend was the way to go.

When the tea had steeped, I brought it over to the table. Edmund was sitting at it now, and the thing didn't shake even when he leaned on it.

"'Tis a simple break at the joint," he said. "A man could mend it in no time at all."

"Not my dad… He can fix people, though."

"A physician, is he?" Edmund asked.

"No. A psychologist. But he's very good at it," I said.

"A psychologist. A beautiful word. What does it mean?"

"I guess you'd call him a soul doctor."

"He must be very holy then," Edmund said.

"Nope. He's just good at fixing other people."

"Mayhap I could mend the table for ye," he said.

"Mom would like that," I said. "Try your tea."

Edmund sipped it.

"Take the bag out first," I said.

He tried a second sip and made a face. "Strange taste. Have ye no beer?"

"How old are you?" I asked him.

"Sixteen, near seventeen."

"You have to be twenty-one to drink beer in California," I said.

"Twenty-one? What the hell for?" he asked. "Are ye savages?"

"Some people start a lot earlier. But it's illegal if you're not an adult. And my mom would kill me if I gave one of my friends beer. How about—wait a minute."

I went to the refrigerator and pulled out a cola. "Try this," I said, and popped the can open.

Edmund tried one sip. Then he tilted back the can and slurped. "Nectar," he said. "What d'ye call it?"

"It's just a cola. Some people call them soft drinks. There's plenty in there. You can pull one out any time you want."

Edmund got up and went over to the fridge. "May I open't?"

"Sure."

He jumped back when the chill air hit him. "'Tis winter in there!"

"Yep," I said. "Refrigeration."

He knelt down and carefully put one hand inside. He felt the food, picked it up and looked at it. Spelled out the words on the packages.

"Is it always so within this chest?" he asked.

"Yeah," I said. "You can adjust the temperature, but that's what it's for. To keep food cold so it doesn't spoil."

"'Tis the wonder of the world," he breathed.

"Wait'll you see television."

"Tell-a-vision?" Edmund said. "Prophecy?"

"Not quite," I said.

"Whatever tell-a-vision be, it must wait—I must ask ye now to lead me to the jakes."

"The what?"

"The jakes. The necessary. The outhouse. Surely ye have one of those."

"Let me show you," I said.

Edmund gulped when he saw the bathroom.

"'Tis like—a sort of temple, so white and set about with basins. It's never a jakes."

"Watch me closely," I said in a voice that I realized probably sounded like a kindergarten teacher's. "You sit on that. It's called the toilet. When you're done you wipe yourself with some of that roll of paper. Then you flush—" I showed him how the handle worked "—and then you wash your hands in the sink. Got it?"

"I'll do me best," Edmund said.

"I'll close the door. But I'll be right outside. Okay?"

"Ah, okay."

I waited in the hall. I heard the sounds of flushing and of water running in the sink.

The door opened.

"Must I really wash me hands every single time?" Edmund asked.

"Of course," I said.

"Feels unnatural."

"Germs."

"What?"

"Didn't Doctor Dee ever tell you anything about germs?" I said.

"Nay, that he did not."

"My mom will explain all about them. And there's something else I just thought of."

"What would that be?" Edmund said.

"We bathe. Every single day. Sometimes more than once."

"What ever for?"

"Again, germs."

"But what if I don't want these germs?" Edmund asked, clearly concerned. "What if I just want to be the way I am?"

"No, Edmund. You don't get germs from bathing. You've

got them already. Bathing every day keeps them down. And germs give you diseases."

"Ye mean like plague?" Edmund asked.

"Yes, exactly like plague," I said.

"And ye've no plague here?"

"Nobody I ever knew or ever heard of has ever had the plague."

Edmund shook his head. "Ye've conquered the plague," he said. "O, brave new world that hath such people in it."

"Mom says soap and water can solve half the problems in the world," I said.

"Very well. I will bathe. Show me what I must do."

"Wait a minute—I am not going to show you how I bathe," I exclaimed.

"I never meant for ye to uncover yourself to me. Just show me the equipments."

"Tub," I said and pointed. "Taps. Hot water. Cold water. This little gizmo closes the tub. Soap. Shampoo for your hair. Washcloth. Towel for drying off after."

Edmund was taking everything in like a dry sponge. He pointed over my head and asked, "What is yon?"

"That's the shower. Some people like showers better than baths."

"And what does it do? Does it bathe ye, too?"

"Yes. It's sort of like standing in the rain, only you can make it the temperature you want."

"I would try it at once," Edmund said. And he twisted the faucets as far as they would go and plunged his hands under the water.

"Great idea," I said. "Hand your clothes out through the door and I'll wash them for you."

"But they're the only clothes I've got," he said.

"I'll find you some others,' I said. "Trust me, Edmund. Nobody wears codpieces any more."

"Very good," he said. "I will fear no evil."

"Just don't be afraid of the soap, either."

I was glad Edmund was being so good about the bath thing. Because he stank. He reeked. It was worse than being with Dad on a three-day camping trip.

I put the smelly tights, shirt, and filthy unmentionables in the wash on gentle, which, since there were no labels with washing instructions, seemed like the safest bet. Then I went back to check on Edmund.

The shower was running full blast, and I could hear him splashing around.

"Everything okay in there?" I shouted.

"Okay, indeed!" he replied. "I'm never coming out."

"I should tell you, the hot water runs out eventually."

"Then I'll come out when it does so," he said. "This is the greatest work of man since the creation. If only Doctor Dee could know of it."

I figured this was a good time to find something to cover him up when he was done. I left him splashing away, went into my mom's bedroom and went through the closet and chest of drawers she'd shared with Dad.

There was quite a bit of his stuff left. He'd been traveling light when he went off to develop as an individual, and I could have dressed Edmund in anything from a three-piece suit (ten years old, but in great shape) to a Moroccan caftan with about a hundred buttons down the front. I decided to go for simple: tan pants, and a polo shirt. I found a belt and some white socks. Nothing would be an exact fit; Dad was taller than Edmund, and Edmund had broader shoulders, but I figured it would get him through till tomorrow. Then Mom and I could get him some stuff.

"Edmund, your clothes are outside the door," I called as I set them down.

"Thank ye, Miranda," he said.

A few minutes later, he came into the living room. He was a shade lighter, and his hair was damp. He'd managed the clothes. The shirt was on all right, and the pants were okay, except that the zipper was down.

"Edmund, that little metal thing down in the front? Pull it up."

It took him three tries. Then he worked the zipper up and down another ten.

"Marvelous strange," he said.

"Are you hungry?" I asked.

"Not a whit. But I would like another cola."

"Help yourself."

On his way to the kitchen, he paused by our flat-screen TV.

"What device is this?" he asked.

"Television," I said. "Get your cola and I'll show you how it works."

I wasn't going to throw Edmund in at the deep end of TV. I had the perfect introduction to the whole concept ready to go. It was a DVD of *Romeo and Juliet.* I'd watched about six productions as part of my preparation for my audition, and this one was ideal for him. The whole thing was staged in Elizabethan costumes and was done on a copy of an Elizabethan stage. And Mr. Gillinger had told us that *R&J* was one of Shakespeare's two most popular plays. Maybe it would turn out Edmund had seen it.

When he came back, I got all teachery. "Now. Edmund, this is television." I turned on the screen. It flared up huge and blue.

Edmund pushed himself into the back of the sofa. His eyes got big.

"What are ye conjurin'?" he said. "Be this some hole like the one I just fell through? Are ye openin' a portal to another world?"

"It's okay. It's just television, and it's just turning on. There are a lot of different things you can do with TV. Right now, we're going to show you a movie. It's also called a DVD. See this little disk? The whole movie is on it. All we do is turn on the television with this thing called a remote, put the DVD in the player like so, turn on the player and then we get this screen that asks us what we want to do. Play movie, select scenes, special features, languages. Anybody can do this. You can do it, too. Ready?"

I put *Romeo and Juliet* into the player.

There were a couple of ads for British movies. They whipped by so fast that Edmund didn't understand anything about them I'm sure. But that wasn't what really confused him. It was the pictures themselves.

"Are these people or spirits?" he asked. "Why be they flat and small? Why do they jerk so, like mad poppets?"

"They're just clips from movies," I said. "To get you to want to watch the whole thing. Don't worry. The thing we're going to see will make sense to you. In fact, you may even have seen it in London."

"I feel like me head's being whirled about by a huracano," he said. He grabbed one of the sofa cushions and held it across his chest. "I do not like this television."

"You'll get used to it," I said. "Everyone does. Now watch."

The screen changed and I hit the play movie button. There was a fanfare of old-fashioned music and the title came on the screen: *Romeo and Juliet* by William Shakespeare.

"Nay," Edmund said. "'Tis never." His jaw dropped; he held his breath.

"'Tis," I said.

The movie started. An actor called Chorus was standing in the middle of the set that was supposed to be a street in Verona. *"Two households both alike in dignity, in fair Verona where we lay our scene—"* he began.

"'Tis never," Edmund repeated.

"From ancient grudge break to new mutiny, where civil blood makes civil hands unclean—"

Edmund made a sound between a scream and a shout. He turned to me, and his face, which had been almost relaxed when he came out of the shower, was full of horror.

"Witch, by what enchantment have ye conjured up me brother William's play?"

Chapter Four

"William Shakespeare is your *brother?*"

"Aye, if my parents are my parents and the world is the world," he said.

"You said your last name was Shakeshaft."

"Shakeshaft, Shakespeare, 'tis the same thing—the family goes by either. I use Shakeshaft to difference me from Will."

I hit the pause button. The Chorus stopped with his mouth open.

"What devilishness is this?" Edmund asked. "What trickery? I thought ye honest, Miranda Hoberman, and kind, too. But now I take ye for a sly witch after all. Did ye pluck yon from my memory? What else have ye taken from me?"

"Edmund," I said. "Get a grip. There's a simple explanation. We're still doing the play. Now. People today."

"Four hundred years and more after we opened it?" Edmund said. "Go to. It isn't that good!"

"We think it is," I said.

"Who thinks so?" Edmund demanded.

"The whole world, pretty much. *Romeo and Juliet* gets

done everywhere. Not just England. Here, too. Russia. Japan. Canada. Everywhere."

"Never."

"Edmund, you know how you think Doctor Dee is the greatest man of the age? Well, that's what most of us think about William Shakespeare. Probably not one person in a hundred now knows anything about John Dee. But everybody knows Shakespeare's name."

Edmund looked totally shocked. "Ye're lying! Ye must be. But why? Why do ye tell me this?"

"I can prove it," I said. "Wait right there."

I went into the little room that Dad had used as his office when he was working out of our home. There were two walls of books in there. One was all his psychology stuff. The other was my mom's. It held her nursing books and a whole lot of stuff on theater. On the bottom shelf on that side was a big red book called *The Riverside Shakespeare.* It had all the plays. I flipped it open to *Romeo and Juliet.*

"Look," I said, and I dumped the book in Edmund's lap. "If you're Edmund Shakeshaft or Shakespeare, and William was your brother, then this is his book. And *Romeo and Juliet's* on page ten fifty-eight."

Edmund touched the title like he couldn't help himself. "The Prologue..." he said. "Enter Chorus..."

Carefully, he turned one page after another. His lips moved. "Sampson. Gregory. Benvolio. Romeo. Mercutio." He went through the play until he came to the last scene. "Aye, 'tis all here, seemingly," he said. "Ye spell passing strangely, howbeit. Every word alike every time."

"We think you spelled strangely," I pointed out.

"But 'twas our language. Ye're only using it," Edmund said. Then he turned back to the beginning of the book. "'Tis a thick volume indeed. What more be in it?"

He studied the pages. Some of these were copied from the First Folio, the original collection of all Shakespeare's plays, back in 1623. "A catalog of the several comedies, histories and tragedies contained in this volume," he read. "Comedies. *The Tempest.* No, he's written no such play."

"Not yet," I said. "We think that was his last one."

"*Two Gentlemen of Verona,* aye," he went on. "*The Merry Wives of Windsor.* That's the new one. *Measure For Measure,* no. *The Comedy of Errors,* yes."

He went through the whole list, going "aye" and "nay." Then he looked at the other pages from the First Folio.

One of these was his brother's portrait, and when he saw it, he hooted.

"Will, ha, ha, 'tis Will. Oh, I wish the fellow could see this picture of himself. Ah, Willy, Willy, ye're four hundred years gone and the whole world thinks this is what ye looked like." He clapped his hands like a little kid.

"What's the matter?" I said.

"Nothing at all—nothing whatever. 'Tis the best of time's revenges. Ah, Willy, Willy, ye pompous fool, I could almost feel sorry for ye."

"Not a good picture, I'm guessing?"

"If ye take away his hair and add a calf's-worth of weight, and a life of years spent in hard drinking, 'tis like enough to him," Edmund said. "But when I saw him Tuesday he was a handsome fellow still, with a full head of hair, and a beard that curled over his jaw, and a jewel hanging from his ear. And very vain he is of his appearance."

"So anyway, now you believe I'm not a witch, or a spirit, or anything but what I said I was, right?" I asked.

"I know nothing for sure any more. Save that in a world where my brother is accounted great and Doctor Dee is forgotten, anything is possible, fair or foul. The seacoast of Bohemia could be no stranger. And Bohemia has never a yard of seacoast."

He put the book on the coffee table. "What more magics will ye show me, Miranda Hoberman?"

"Would you like to see the rest of the play?" I said.

"I would not," he said. "'Tis too unnatural watching the poppets do it."

"You probably saw it done in London, huh?"

"I have been in it. Will is not the only actor in the family."

"You're kidding," I said. "Who did you play?"

"'Twas three years ago, so there was only one part I could play, of course," Edmund said. "Juliet."

"You are kidding me," I said.

"I am what?"

"You actually played Juliet?"

"The first time anyone ever did. Since my voice changed, I've done some of the servants, and the Count Paris. Last time I did the Chorus, as well."

"Ever play Romeo?" I asked.

"Ha! As if Dick Burbage would let anyone else play him," he snorted. "Will did it once when Burbage was sick, and Burbage still hasn't forgiven him. Not that Will gives a fart. But little a chance has any hired actor of playing such a role as that. Not unless the play be done a good long way from London where the Lord Chamberlain's Men will never hear of it until 'tis too late."

I knew some of what he was talking about. Gillinger had made us study some background material on Shakespeare's times. Richard Burbage was the leading actor in the Lord Chamberlain's Men, which was also the acting company Shakespeare belonged to. The plays he wrote were their property, but other acting companies would steal a popular play if they could get away with it. And *Romeo and Juliet* had been very popular.

"You know," I said, "I just read for Juliet this afternoon."

Edmund shook his head. "Ye did what for her?"

"I read for the part. We're doing it here, in town."

"But girls cannot appear on stage. 'Twould be filthy."

"No it isn't. I know you guys used guys to play girls all the time. But we think that's weird. There's nothing wrong with having girls play girls."

"Women on the stage. 'Tis something too French," Edmund said.

"Well, maybe the French are just smarter than you English," I said. "Anyway, there's a lot of great English actresses now."

"Even in England they do this?" Edmund said.

"Yep. That version of *Romeo and Juliet* I tried to show you has women playing all the women's parts. Juliet, the Nurse, Lady Capulet, Romeo's mother. And I'll tell you something else. In our production some of the servants will probably be played by girls playing guys. 'Cause guys don't come out for drama much."

Edmund shook his head again. "'Tis strange. 'Tis mickle strange. Me best role ever, played by—a woman."

"You know," I said, "we've been talking a long time. Would you like dinner?"

"I do not feel hungry," he said. "But perhaps I should eat."

"Let me introduce you to the great American hamburger."

Edmund followed me out to the kitchen. He followed every move I made with the attention of a hawk. The whole cooking thing fascinated him.

"'Tis all familiar and yet not," he said. "This, more than

yon television makes it seem as though I am a stranger in a strange land."

I made us each two hamburgers with buns and all the agricultural trimmings. I didn't want to trust the broken table with food on it, so we went into the living room again and sat down at the coffee table with our plates and glasses of milk.

Edmund watched everything I did, and copied it.

"Meat's fresh," he said chewing his first bite of burger. "Who does your slaughtering?"

"The store. We buy all our food at the store. I've never killed an animal in my life. Except flies and stuff. Have you?"

Edmund laughed. "My family are glovers," he began. "There's not a calf in Stratford safe from us. My brother Gilbert's the best of us, though. Fast and neat, that's Gilbert's way. Will, for his part, would often make a speech in high style to the poor beast before he did the deed. 'Tis said he was hoping to bore the little fellow to death and spare them the knife thereby." He tried the milk and smacked his lips. "Fresh, though it lacks body. Ye say ye have no cow of your own?"

"No cow, no calves, no garden, either," I said. "Most people today buy their food."

"'Tis as if ye're waited on by spirits.... Invisible spirits."

"Not really," I said.

When dinner was over, I checked on Edmund's laundry. I put everything on air dry. I was pretty sure heat would shrink those tights of his.

And of course he was fascinated by the washing machine and the dryer.

"Have all of ye such things?" he asked.

"Pretty much. If people don't, they go to a laundromat and get their stuff done there."

"Next ye'll be telling me ye can all fly!"

Right on cue, I heard the heavy thumping of a helicopter passing overhead.

"Come on outside," I said. "Got something to show you."

We went and stood in our front yard.

At first, Edmund didn't seem to understand what he was seeing. He crossed his arms, cocked his head and watched as though his eyes couldn't quite focus on it. Then the copter curved around heading back the way it had come, and Edmund ducked back under our tree.

"Is it perilous?" he asked. "D'ye think it saw us?"

"It's just a TV station's news helicopter. It's not interested in us. It's probably out doing traffic reports."

"Do men ride such things?" Edmund asked, mouth in a perfect *O*.

"And women, too," I said.

Then a car went by, too fast, like most of the cars that use our street. It was a sports car of some kind and made a hell of a racket.

Edmund yelped, and ducked behind the tree. "And what was *that?*"

"A car," I said. "And yes, most people have them. Sometimes more than one."

"A car. Damned bland name for a demon thing like that. Have ye such a device?"

"We do, but it's at work. My mom drives it. I know how, but I'm too young yet. I mean, I'm old enough, sixteen. But the insurance is so high for a young driver that we can't afford it."

"What makes it go?" Edmund asked.

"Gasoline."

"Another word I never heard..." He came out from behind the tree and looked up and down the street. There were cars in driveways, cars at the curb. He studied them for a few minutes, then bent down and touched the pavement. "Hard."

The street seemed to interest him more than the cars. He kept rubbing his hands across the asphalt, picking up bits of gravel and studying them. When he was done, he turned around and faced the house.

"A house I know," he said. "And grass I know. And a tree, though 'tis a kind I've never seen before. Windows with glass, but such great panes of it. And flowers, though I know not their names. But all else is like an enchantment. I understand none of it."

"Maybe you'd like to take a walk," I said. "Get a little more oriented."

"Oriented," Edmund said slowly.

"Sorry. Is that another word you don't know?"

"Doctor Dee do have some old maps," Edmund said. "He turns them to the east, toward Jerusalem. He calls that orienting."

"Well Malpaso Row is east of us. So I guess it's the same thing," I said.

"Aye," Edmund said after a moment of silence. "Come then, Miranda Hoberman, and orient me."

I locked the house and we headed down the street. Malpaso Row was on the other side of the freeway from our neighborhood. Only a few blocks away, but totally different from our quiet, boring avenue. It was the newest shopping center in town, very high-concept. It had buildings designed to look like a neighborhood in Italy, with pricey apartments above the stores, fountains and things like that.

We walked slowly, Edmund taking in every detail of the

houses and yards we passed. Then we turned a few corners and were in the middle of a whole new world.

My first problem was getting Edmund to cross the freeway overpass. It wasn't the height that bothered him. It was the sight of all the cars below us, hood to trunk with their lights on, and even more the roar that came up from the eight lanes of traffic under our feet.

"This howling, this howling, how d'ye stand it?" he shouted to me, clapping his hands over his ears.

"Edmund, it's okay," I said. "It's just rush hour. Every one of those cars has somebody in it who's just trying to get home. It's not dangerous. It's normal."

"'Tis hellish."

"Well, okay. We don't have to do this now," I said. "We can go back to the house if you want to."

I could tell that was exactly what Edmund wanted to do. But he wouldn't let himself. "I must bear it," he said. "Lead on."

So we crossed the overpass. Then I had to explain to him about stoplights and crosswalks and taking turns. This was after he stepped out in front of a line of cars turning into the main drag of Malpaso Row from a left-turn lane and he nearly got creamed.

A driver shouted, "Watch it, you stupid bastard!"

And Edmund shouted back, "Ye're the whoreson heir of a mongrel bitch, an eater of broken meats and the very flower of the pox!"

"No, Edmund!" I yelled at him. "No, no, no, no, no! Never when the light is red. Only when the light is green. And stay between the nice straight white lines. That's how it works."

"Must I wait the pleasure of some lantern to do as I wish

about so small a thing as cross?" he said. "'Tis like a prison to walk your streets."

"You'll live a lot longer if you do," I said, calming down.

"What of the yellow light?" he said.

"That means, 'caution'."

"Aha. So a man has some choice at least."

"Come on," I said. "You've survived your first stoplight. Let's see what other trouble you can get into."

Chapter Five

We cruised slowly up and down past the clothing stores and the restaurants and the bars. Edmund paused at one that had a sign hanging out that said:

Falstaff's
A Traditional
English Pub

"Can we not go in here, at least?" he begged.

"Edmund, we're underage. They'd throw us out so fast you'd meet yourself coming in. They'd lose their license if they let us stay."

"Monstrous. Unnatural. Wrong."

"Come on," I said. "Let me show you something you'll like."

Down at the end of the street was a Corners Books. I was pretty sure Edmund would be interested in it. And it turned out he was.

"Books," he said, like he might have said "Jewels."

It was a big two-story place with a coffee bar in the middle of the ground floor. We walked around every section, taking it just as slow as Edmund wanted.

"So many, so many," he kept repeating.

He took some of them off the shelves, touching them as if he thought they might evaporate under his hands, studying the way they were made.

"Paper's different," he said. "Aye, and the bindings. But what riches ye have, Miranda. Even in London there's no such place as this."

Finally we ended up in the magazine section, which was right next to the coffee. The magazines absolutely transfixed Edmund. Or anyway, the covers did.

"Such images. How d'ye ever..." he breathed as he looked at all the bright-color pics of cars, pretty girls and famous heads.

But before I could display my vast erudition again, there was a voice behind us.

"Hey, Miri. What's up?"

I turned around and saw Bobby Ruspoli smiling at me.

"Hey, dude," I said.

Edmund also turned.

"Bobby, this is my cousin Ed," I said quickly, and feeling rather proud of myself for being such an adroit thinker. "He's from England."

"Hey, Ed," Bobby said.

"Give ye good even."

"Ed, this is Bobby Ruspoli from school," I said.

"You guys busy?" Bobby asked.

"Not exactly," I said.

"Then come on over and help me work on Drew. I'm trying to talk him into reading tomorrow. Stubborn geek says he doesn't want to be on stage."

I would have agreed in a ten-thousandth of a second, if I'd been alone. But I had Mr. Shakeshaft to consider. "What do you think, is it okay, Ed?"

"Yes. It is okay," Edmund said.

So Bobby led us over to his table and we sat down with Drew.

"Hey, Drew," I said.

"Hi, Miranda."

He had an empty espresso cup in front of him, and a paperback copy of the play.

"Drew, this is my cousin Ed, Edmund, from England," I said. "Edmund, this is Drew Jenkins. He's in school with me, too."

"Give ye good e'en," Edmund said.

And Drew smiled and said, "Give ye good e'en, as well, fair sir."

"Ye speak English," Edmund said.

"Fairly well for an American," Drew said, and the three Americans laughed.

"Bobby says he wants you to read for the play," I said.

"No way in hell."

"Please," I said. "We need guys."

"You need *actors,*" Drew said. "That lets me out."

"Drew, there were guys on that stage today you could act the asses off of," Bobby said.

"I agree there were some dreadful impersonations of acting," Drew said. "But the fact that they were god-awful doesn't make me good."

"Dude, you have got to get over seventh grade," Bobby said.

"Shut up—"

"This guy," Bobby said, "used to do shows with me all the time in grade school. He was the beautiful white pony. I was the blue car smooth and shiny as satin. That was second grade—"

"Third. Second grade I was the woodcutter and you were the prince."

"Oh, yeah," Bobby said. "But the point is, he was good. Then in seventh grade—"

"Shut up, Bobby. Nobody cares what happened in seventh grade."

"Apparently *you* do," Bobby said.

"Okay, I do. So shut up about it," Drew said.

"We were both cast in the Children's Musical Theater Holiday Spectacular," Bobby went on. "You didn't know Drew could sing, right? Well, he can. Better than me. And he got a solo. 'Christmas Is a Time of Giving,' right at the end of act one. I mean, it's the big act finisher, right? And he dries up. Can't remember his song. Just stands there and—"

"Shut. Up. Now," Drew said.

"All I'm saying is, it's time to get back on the horse, Drew. The beautiful white pony. It's been four years."

"And all I'm saying is, you're wrong. It's not that I'm scared. Scarred for life, definitely. But not scared. I'm just not interested."

"Miri," Bobby said. "Explain to him why he's interested."

"I can't," I said. "But, Drew. Cast parties."

"I come to those anyway," Drew said.

Which was true. Whenever there was a cast party and Bobby showed up, Drew was with him. This was whether Bobby had a girl on his arm or not.

"They're more fun when you've just finished a show," I said hopefully.

"I have all the fun I can stand at them now," Drew said. "Any more fun, I'd die from sheer pleasure."

"Please," I said. "We need people."

"No."

Edmund picked up Drew's script. "I see ye have marked Mercutio's speeches," he said. "Friar Lawrence's, too. Why have ye done so if ye are not interested?"

"I've been helping him," Drew said. "We've been running lines for weeks."

"I could see ye as Mercutio," Edmund said. "Friar Lawrence, too, though ye be something too young. 'Twould depend on who else was in the company."

"Ed's an actor," I said. "A real one."

"Hey," Bobby said. "You ever play in this thing?"

"Yes. Okay. I have," Edmund said.

"What part?" Bobby asked.

"Different ones. I've played in it more than once. But tell me, what part do ye fancy for yourself?"

"Romeo," Bobby said like there was no question about it.

"Romeo," Edmund mused. "It would not be my first thought for ye."

"Oh? Who would you cast me as?"

"Tybalt, mayhap, if ye can fence well," Edmund said.

"Tybalt's not a very big part," Bobby said.

"Thirty-five lines," Drew said. "But he's on a lot."

"Not a long part," Edmund agreed. "But a large one. He tries to kill Romeo at old Capulet's party. Later, he kills Mercutio. Thus Romeo slays him, and must flee Verona. If there were no Tybalt, ye'd have no tragedy and Romeo and Juliet would live to ripe old ages."

"Well, anyway, I'm up for Romeo."

Edmund turned to Drew. "Tell me, fellow. When ye went dry onstage when ye were a lad, what happened next?"

"What do you mean, what happened next?" Drew said. "Nothing happened."

"What nothing?" Edmund persisted.

"I just stood there until I started crying. Then they pulled the curtain."

"Horrible. D'ye mean no one came to your aid?" Edmund asked. "No fellow-actor came and said, aught like, 'Will you not give us a song?' or somewhat like that?"

"We were just kids. Nobody thought to do anything."

"Would that happen now, d'ye think?" Edmund asked.

"Never," Bobby said.

"No way," I said. "We'd be there for each other."

Drew shrugged. "Look, I'm not being neurotic about something that happened when I was twelve. I'm just not interested anymore. Walking on stage, reciting lines. The same lines every night. It gets old real fast."

"Is that what ye think acting is?" Edmund said.

"It's all I know about it," Drew said. "If you even call it acting."

"Then ye do well to stay away from it—for 'tis nothing of the kind."

"I'm always finding new stuff to do," Bobby said.

"And ye, cousin Miranda," Edmund said. "What is acting to you?"

"It's hard to say," I said. "But it's the most important thing in my life."

Edmund scratched his beard and looked up. "For me," he began, "acting is queen, mother and mistress all in one. And more than a bit of a bitch. But I love her as I love no other thing. But, no. That does not speak to what acting is. Acting is—is finding the truth in the most artificial thing there is. For theater is a metaphor for all of life and all that is truest in it. Acting an endless race through a hall of mirrors seeking the one that shows, not yourself, but the truth of the character you're playing. The truth in the shadow. And then reflects it, not to yourself, but to the audience at your feet. And when it works, there is nothing finer."

"Man," Bobby said. "I mean, word, dude."

"I do not take your meanin', friend."

"He means you really told the truth about it," I said.

Drew picked up the script and pondered the cover. It showed a balcony with the doors behind it open and light streaming through them. Romeo was in silhouette below, but the balcony was empty. No Juliet. We all had the same copy of the play. I thought it was a really stupid picture. Juliet was supposed to already be on the balcony when Romeo showed up. This cover looked like whoever'd done it hadn't even read the play.

But now Drew was staring at it like it meant something to him. "I wonder if I could do that," he said. "You do make a guy want to try."

"What part do ye favor?" Edmund asked.

"I don't think it matters," Drew replied. "As long as I could have some of that feeling you were talking about."

"'Tis hard to do. 'Tis not to be counted upon. But mayhap I could help ye toward it if ye would like."

"Yeah. I would."

Bobby burst into the conversation, excited. "Cool. Drew reads tomorrow, he scores a part, and Ed coaches him. Ruspoli and Jenkins together again, live on stage. Thanks, Ed!"

"Listening to meself, I wish—Cousin Miranda, may I not read tomorrow?"

"Do it, man," Bobby said. "It'd be so cool to have a real English dude in the play."

I felt a whoosh of panic. *No, no, no, Edmund must not read. Edmund must not be cast. Edmund must be hidden away.* But then

I thought how stupid that was, and, really, how impossible. For better or worse, Edmund Shakeshaft was living in California, in this century, in my house, and he'd have to find a way to fit in. And maybe being part of the one thing he'd learned how to do in his own time that we were still doing in this time would help him to adjust.

"Yeah," I said, though still a little weakly. "Tryouts are two-thirty tomorrow after school."

"I will come then."

"Okay," I said, thinking that in one way at least this could end up being the most accurate *Romeo and Juliet* anybody had done in more than four hundred years.

Bobby and Drew started asking Edmund all kinds of questions about what it was like to be an actor in England. And I was really impressed with how he managed to answer them without giving anything away.

"How long have you been acting?"

"Oh, since I left school."

"How many shows have you done?"

"I don't recall for certain. About fifty, I think."

"Have you done much TV?"

"Television? Nay. I do not think I would like to do it."

I kept thinking I ought to drag him away, but he seemed to be enjoying playing with the guys, and they were definitely interested in what he had to say. Finally, Edmund solved my dilemma for me.

"Cuz," he said. "I am weary. Can we not go home?"

"Sure," I said.

"Would you like a lift?" Drew asked.

"We're close," I said.

"Come on," Bobby said. "Drew's got a new ride."

"It's okay. We'll just walk," I said.

But Edmund was suddenly alert. "This ride ye speak of, friend Drew. Is it a car?"

"Sure," Drew said.

"I would like to ride in it."

I think he was trembling just a little.

"I call shotgun," Bobby said.

Drew's new car was an old car. A bug-eyed little thing that looked like clowns might burst out of it at any minute. I'd never seen anything like it.

"What is this?" I asked.

Drew smiled. "A Citroën 2CV. The most flawless meld of engineering requirements ever designed to run on gas. Intended to take French farmers out of the age of the horse and put them behind the wheel. Totally simple, modular construction. If you dent a fender, you unbolt it and slap on a new one. The backseat lifts out for cargo. The same cable that runs the speedometer runs the windshield wiper. And you can carry a bushel of eggs across a plowed field without cracking one. That was part of the design requirement. I love that about it."

"And it can hit forty-five without even trying," Bobby said.

"Actually, this is the last model. It's capable of sixty-two."

It also had a canvas top that slid along the roofline. Not really a convertible, but the same effect.

"Drop that top!" Bobby demanded, and he and Drew unlatched the canvas and pushed it back.

The little coffee-grinder engine started up and we bounced out of the parking lot and onto the street.

I could sense Edmund tensing up beside me. Being so small ourselves made all the SUVs and vans seem even bigger than they really were, and having the top down made them very, very close. But it was the speed that seemed to bother him most.

Not that Drew was speeding. We were doing thirty-five, which was totally legal on that street, but it did feel faster than it would have in a regular car with the wind in our faces, plus Edmund's long hair was whipping around.

Edmund was pushing himself back into the seat the way he had when he was watching television, and his face was set like he was a sea captain on an old-time ship staring into the storm. He looked handsome as hell and vulnerable as a little kid all at the same time.

Then his hand grabbed mine and held it like he was never letting go.

"Ah!" I went, because it hurt and I was surprised.

"What?" Bobby said, looking back over his shoulder.

"Nothing. I just like Drew's ride, that's all," I said, and I squeezed Edmund's hand back.

That squeeze ran all the way up my arm and into my heart.

Uh-oh. This should not be happening, I thought. *Must not happen.*

But I couldn't just let go of his hand. I held on to it all the way home.

Chapter Six

Drew pulled into our driveway. Bobby got out and opened the door for us. I crawled out of the back seat, but Edmund unfolded himself and climbed over the side of the car. Then he leaned on it casually, but I was pretty sure his legs were trembling and he needed the support. I walked around and took his arm.

"I thank ye, friend," he said to Drew. "A most excellent ride."

"Any time."

"Well, good night," I broke in. "See you at tryouts."

"Cool," Bobby said, and got back in with Drew.

Edmund and I waved as they took off down our dark street.

When we couldn't hear the engine of the Citroën anymore, Edmund barfed all over the lawn. Then he allowed himself to collapse onto the driveway.

"Dear God, do ye do that all the time?" he asked, looking up at me. "'Twas like being on a mad horse with no reins. Or a plunging ship with a gale blowing. How d'ye stand such a thing?"

"Edmund, it's okay," I said, sitting down beside him. "Really. Drew's a good driver. There was nothing wrong. Cars are the best way anybody's ever come up with for getting from one place to another."

"How fast were we *going?*"

"About thirty-five."

"Thirty-five *what?*"

"Miles an hour."

"Thirty-five miles an hour?" Edmund said. "How is it we're still alive?"

"Maybe you'll like riding in our car better," I said. "It's bigger and safer."

"My car riding days are over!"

"They can't be," I said. "Everyone takes cars everywhere. You'll get over being afraid. And I'll tell you something else. Sooner or later, you're going to be driving."

"No! Such a thing...d'ye think I could learn the manage of a car?" Edmund asked.

"I think you could do anything you wanted to." I said it just to cheer him up. But when I said it, I realized that I meant it.

"I, do such a thing," Edmund said. "It must be easier than it looks."

"We'd better go in."

It was still early, only a little after nine o'clock, but tucking Edmund into bed in the extra room seemed like the best thing to do with him at this point. I needed some private time to sort out a couple of things. Such as how I was going to explain to Mom that we had a new, permanent houseguest. And why my heart was still going thumpity thump.

And Edmund really was tired. "Saint Mary and Joseph,

I am weary and 'tis late for a night with no ranging to be done," he said. "Miranda, where may a poor player lay his head?"

I showed him the bedroom. But then there was another little problem.

"Edmund," I said. "What do you sleep in?"

He thumped the bed and looked surprised at how much it bounced. "Oh. On such a warm night as this, I'll need nothing. Thank you, Miranda."

"Okay," I said. "But if you have to—go to the jakes in the middle of the night—"

"I will cover myself up. I *do* have a proper sense of shame."

"Well, good, then. Good night."

"Miranda, before we say good-night, will ye pray with me?" Edmund asked.

"Uh…yeah. Okay, I guess," I said. "What religion are you?"

"Church of England, of course," he said. "Inclining more toward the old faith than some, as I expect ye've noted. What are ye?"

Dad was Jewish, and Mom wasn't anything. My six-week stint in Sunday school had been because I was curious where some of my friends went on Sunday morning back in the second grade. My curiosity had been satisfied and I hadn't been back since.

"Sort of nothing," I said. "But I'll pray with you if you want me to."

"Were ye never baptized, then?"

"Nope."

"Kneel down with me, Miranda Hoberman," Edmund said. "And do as I do."

And just like a little kid he knelt down beside his bed, crossed himself, folded his hands and bowed his head.

"Dear God, 'tis Edmund Shakeshaft, a sinner. I am heartily sorry for taking part in Doctor Dee's necromantic experiment today. And I am justly punished by being ripped away from all that I have known. But Ye have shown me great mercy, Dear Lord, in sending me to this place so full of wonders and granting me this marvelous girl as my help and companion. I know not what tomorrow may bring, or even what may hap tonight. But I confide in Your mercy to see me safely through. And if it be Your will that stranger things may yet befall, yet will I repose my hope in Ye. Bless Miranda Hoberman, and grant her the desire of her heart, as ye granted mine, that she may play Juliet. Bless Drew Jenkins and Bobby Ruspoli and grant them safe passage home in yon car. Bless all at home, Mother, Father, Joan, Gilbert, Richard, Anne and her young ones Susannah, Hamlet and Judith. And even my brother Will, whom Ye know to be a horse's ass." He looked over at me and whispered, "Is there aught else ye'd like to add?"

"I'm good," I said. "Wrap it up."

"Your meaning?" Edmund whispered again.

"Finish whenever you're ready," I said, realizing that I was whispering, too.

"Then in the name of Your Son, our Savior Jesus Christ who lives and reigns with Ye and the Holy Spirit, Amen."

"Amen, too." I got up. "Good night," I said.

"Give ye good rest, Miranda," Edmund said.

I closed the door behind me and went out into the living room.

I thought about watching something or listening to something, but I realized that what I really wanted was quiet. No, not wanted. Needed. All in all, this had been a pretty unusual Tuesday, and I had a lot to process.

So I sat in the big armchair that had been Dad's and would

be again if he ever came back, and closed my eyes and tried to meditate.

The thing is, I can't meditate. Either I start thinking about random stuff, or I fall asleep. I don't know how the Dalai Lama does it.

So I just sat there, and when I couldn't meditate, I went to bed and thought.

First of all, how could I make my mom believe any of this? I couldn't, I realized. But Edmund could. As soon as she'd been around him for ten minutes, she'd see that I was telling the truth. Once she knew that, her nurse self would kick in, and she'd do whatever she could to help him.

Second, why was my hand still tingling a little?

I worked on that one until I fell asleep.

Chapter Seven

There were three things Mom insisted on for me before I started classes: breakfast, bath and the value of an invigorating walk to school. And she always made sure that I was clean, fed and out the door on time no matter how many shifts she'd pulled the day before. My life was as orderly as she could make it. I feared I was about to mess with that big time.

When Mom strode in the door at seven-thirty the next morning, I was waiting for her. "Hi, honey. Look at this. Actually crossing paths with you. I could get used to it."

"Mom, sit down. I've got something to tell you," I replied.

"Don't you have school?"

"I do. But this is important," I said.

"Can I get my shower first, at least?" Mom asked.

"Good idea," I said. "In fact, great idea."

"Uh-oh," she said. "If you think a shower is going to help that much, I'd better hear this now."

"Good thinking," I said.

Mom put her chin in her hand and listened to me, leaning

on our broken table, while I told her the whole story, including hanging out with Bobby and Drew, and Edmund barfing on our lawn. Even in scrubs, after sixteen hours of work, my fifty-year-old mother was beautiful. Her long straight nose and her big gray eyes comforted me in a way nothing else could have. And I knew I was wrong; Mom did believe me. I could tell it from her face.

When I was done, she studied me long and hard. "You know, I saw a UFO once," she said.

"You never told me that."

"It was funny," Mom said. "I was driving to L.A. on Highway 60, and the guy I was with said, 'Look isn't that a UFO?' and there, hanging over the freeway, was this beautiful thing. It had a shiny coppery bottom and a silver dome that seemed to be shining emerald light through a row of windows. I looked for wings, but there weren't any, or rotors like a helicopter's. But there weren't any of those, either. Then we drove right under it, and I stuck my head out the side window and looked back and it was gone."

"Wow," I said. "You had a close encounter. You could have seen aliens."

"The point is, Miranda, I saw a UFO once and I still don't believe in them." Mom shook her head. "I mean, I know I had an experience. But how to interpret that experience is something I've never even tried to figure out. That's kind of how I feel right now." She rubbed one hand over the back of the other slowly. "I know you're not lying. Apart from anything else, you never would. And if you ever did, you'd come up with something much more believable. So if you say there's a boy asleep in our guestroom who's William Shakespeare's kid brother, then there is. But I still don't know what to do with that."

I watched her rub her hand back and forth.

"Well, I suppose the first best thing to do is let him sleep," Mom said. "Then, when he wakes up, we'll decide what we have to do next. We'll figure it out. Whatever *it* is." She shook her head. "I wish your father were here. We could really use some of his off-the-wall psychological expertise right now."

Then she went and had her shower.

I sat there listening to her finish bathing. I thought about what she'd said about that strange moment when she'd seen something in the sky that was absolutely not like anything else she'd ever seen.

Yes, Edmund was a UFO. But he wasn't an alien. Not to me.

When Mom came back into the kitchen I saw she was wearing sweats, which was not usual. I figured that with a strange man in the house she was making sure she was well covered up.

Edmund came into the kitchen carrying *The Riverside Shakespeare* in his hand. He was wearing the clothes I'd washed for him.

"I woke early and thought it a good time to read... Oh! Give ye god den, lady." He bowed deeply to Mom.

"Good morning," Mom said. "Miranda has told me about you. Welcome."

"Ye are very good. How may I serve ye?"

"Just sit down and I'll make you breakfast," Mom said.

My Edmund-related tinglies were coming back. I thought how nice it would be to spend the day with him—and besides, I was already missing first period.

"You know," I said, "I could stay home today. I mean, I could help you two get to know each other better."

"Then you would not be able to go to tryouts this afternoon," Mom said.

"Oh. You could lie for me. Just call the office and tell them I'm sick."

"No. I could not. Eat. Get going. Edmund and I will be fine. I'll bring him to school on my way to work so he can go to tryouts with you."

I would have given my right arm to stay home that morning. If I hadn't needed it to play Juliet. I didn't hear a word that was said in any of my classes between homeroom bell and AP English, last period. All I kept thinking about was Mom and Edmund. How were they getting along? What were they talking about? And, more than once, what had it been like for *him* holding my hand last night? I had hardly any time left over to obsess about being Juliet.

I saw Drew in English. It was the only class he and I had together. Drew was in AP everything, and was taking classes at Guadalupe Community College on Tuesdays and Thursdays.

"Enjoyed meeting your cousin last night," he said. "Neat guy."

"He liked you, too."

"Is he really coming to tryouts?" Drew asked.

"Mom's bringing him," I said.

"Cool. Where in England is he from, exactly?"

"Oh, Warwickshire. But he lives in London now."

"I was wondering about his accent," Drew said. "Didn't sound very contemporary."

"Well, that's just the way that branch of the family talks. They're a little old-fashioned."

"Warwickshire… Shakespeare's neck of the woods. Is he from around Stratford?"

"Matter of fact, he is," I said. "How did you know?"

"Well," Drew said. "It's just that my mom and I went

there a few years ago, and I didn't hear anybody with an accent quite like that. Of course we were only there a couple of days."

"I guess it's some kind of family tradition to talk like that," I said quickly. "Most people don't."

"Really neat."

"So are you really coming to tryouts?" I said to change the subject.

"I said I was," Drew said, as if that settled it.

"What part are you reading for?"

"I'm going to try for Mercutio," Drew said. "Edmund said he could see me as either him or Friar Lawrence, and I don't like Friar Lawrence. But I'd better not get it. Not if Gillinger knows what's good for his show."

"Why are you reading for it if you don't want it?"

"I didn't say I didn't want it. It's my favorite part. I just don't think I'd be very good."

Then the bell rang and we all settled down to another forty-five minutes on the burning issue of symbolism in *The Great Gatsby*.

When the bell rang again, I practically flew out of my seat.

Tryouts! Yes! Edmund! Yes! Yes! Now!

"See you!" I said to Drew over my shoulder, and ran out to look for Edmund.

Mom was waiting with him in front of the school. She smiled and waved.

"We have had a most excellent day, cuz," Edmund shouted as I skipped toward them. "We have talked of a world of things. She knows so much."

"It's been enchanting," Mom said. "Of course it started with your enchantment, so that's only logical. But get this—

the hospital called and offered me the day shift. Just like that. No more swing or graveyard after today. I think maybe this guy is good luck."

"We mended the table together," Edmund said. "She showed me the manage of the lawn mower, as well. I am to stay and become son and brother to ye." And he slung arms around Mom and me. "'Tis hard to credit, to lose one family yesterday and gain a new one in a day. But this place is magical."

Ah. "Brother." Not good. On the other hand, Edmund stays. Very good, I thought.

"I knew you'd like him, Mom."

"Like him? Yeah, I like him," she said, giving him a hug back. "It'll be nice to have a little testosterone around the place again."

"Well, we'd better get to tryouts," I said.

"We read lines together this afternoon," Edmund said. "I was Romeo, she was Juliet, and Lady Montague and even Mercutio to me. I was wrong. Women can act. I'd be proud to be on any stage with ye, Ms. Hoberman."

"Ms.?" I said. "You learn fast."

"He does. He's already not the same boy he was this morning."

Edmund beamed. "If there's one thing being a player will teach ye, it is how to acquire new knowledge swiftly. Come, sister. Let me show ye what I've kenned today."

"Sister." Oh, no, no, no, no. Got to do something about that.

"Follow me unto the waiting stage," I said. "But don't call me sister. People around here know I'm an only child."

"Ah, ye're right," Edmund said. "I must call ye cuz, then."

Better than sister at least.

The walk across campus amazed him. He stared at the

thousand students coming and going, laughing and shouting, heading for cars or buses, heading home on foot.

"There are so many of ye, boys and girls together, and so many different kinds and colors. 'Tis as if all Europe, Africa and the Indies have congregated here. There's been nothing like it since the world began, I vow."

"That's basically what's happened," I said. "Plus, we've got a few other kinds you haven't heard of yet."

"And the girls are so lovely. Ye all have all your teeth."

I laughed because what he said surprised me. But I had noticed that Edmund was missing a tooth or two. Fortunately, they were not involved in his smile.

"Lovely," he said. "Ye are all lovely."

"Careful, Edmund. Or you'll have half the school hitting on you. Some of the guys, too."

"Hitting me? For praising their beauty?" Edmund said.

"Hitting *on* you. You know—trying to get to know you way better. As in, carnally."

"It *is* like London, then," Edmund said. He smiled, and I wished for a second that his smile did have a few teeth missing where they showed.

We crossed the lobby and entered the sweet darkness of the theater. I saw Drew and Bobby down front, and a couple of other guys that I didn't already know. There were some new girls there, too. I hoped they were not there to read for Juliet, or that if they were, that at least they couldn't speak English. Anyway, we had some new blood for Gillinger to shed.

Tanya Blair, the plump blonde senior who was Gillinger's assistant director, came toward us with her clipboard. "Here. Fill this out quick," she said, handing Edmund a tryout sheet. Then she leaned her face into mine. "Gorgeous. If he tries to leave, tackle him."

"Right," I said.

I handed Edmund my pen and showed him how to click the little button to make the point appear.

He gasped when he touched the pen to the paper and the ink flowed. "If Will had had one of these he'd likely have written six folios."

But even if Edmund's pen was modern, his writing was as old-school as it gets. I watched as he filled out the form in a style that went back more than four hundred years.

NAME: Edmund Shakeshaft.
AGE: Sixteen, near seventeen.
EDUCATION: I did attend the grammar school at Stratford.
HEIGHT: near six feet.
WEIGHT: Ten stone and two pound.
HAIR: Yes.

"They mean, 'What color?'" I whispered.

Edmund added, "Of a reddish hue."

SKIN:

"What should I put down here?" he asked me.

"Say, 'Ruddy'," I told him.

PREVIOUS CREDITS:

"And what does that mean?"

"What other parts have you played?"

So, next to PREVIOUS CREDITS, Edmund wrote "I did enact the part of Wagner in a *Doctor Faustus* which the Lord Admiral's Men did present privily to divers gentlemen of worship Martinmas last. I did perform also First Citizen, a Welsh Lord and Second Assassin in *Ye Tragedy of Caratacys.* Not long ago, I perform'd Doctor Pinch in *Ye Comedy of Errors,* and smaller parts, as well." He went on and listed about fifty plays. Toward the end he put "*The Tragedy of Romeo and Juliet,* in which I did enact Juliet. That is all I can recall now, but there have been more."

"You know Gillinger is never going to believe you," I said. "No one would believe you."

"And what is a Gillinger?"

"The director."

"The what?"

"The guy who controls the whole production," I said. "He casts it, and tells everyone else what to do. How to act, costumes, lighting, sound. Everything."

"Mayhap he will not, but I will not put down nothing," Edmund said. "And your Gillinger can credit it or not. I ask but the chance to read Romeo this day."

And next to PART(S) FOR WHICH YOU ARE READING he wrote "Romeo."

He carried the sheet to Tanya.

"Why do ye need such a one as this Gillinger?" Edmund asked, when he came back to me. "In London, we–"

But Gillinger's voice came booming through the shadowy theater. "May we have quiet please? I want to begin."

And suddenly a wall came down in front of Edmund's face. It was like I wasn't there anymore. He stared toward the stage, alert and tense, like a dog hoping to be taken on a walk.

"I will begin with the new people," Gillinger said. "Drew Jenkins and—Edmund Shakeshaft—read act two scene four with Bobby Ruspoli. Jenkins, read Mercutio, Bobby read Romeo. Shakeshaft, read Benvolio."

There was practically nothing for Edmund to do. This bit is all Mercutio's. Benvolio has three short lines, great stuff like "Here comes Romeo. Here comes Romeo." And his first line, "Why what is this Tybalt?"

Drew answered:

"More than Prince of Cats, I can tell you. Oh, he is
The courageous captain of compliments. He fights
As you sing prick-song, keeps time, distance, and
Proportion; he rests his minim rests, one, two, and the
Third in your bosom: the very butcher of a silk button,
A duelist; a duelist, a gentleman of the very first
House, of the first and the second cause. Ah, the
Immortal *passado*, the *punto reverso*, the *hay*-"

Drew was really laying it down. Tybalt is a guy who'll pick a fight for anything, which was apparently a compliment of some sort. And he's really good at three things you can do with a sword—the passado, the punto reverso and the hay—all the better to skewer you. The Prince of Cats thing is a joke, the kind Mercutio is always making. In Shakespeare's time there was supposed to be a Prince of Cats and his name was Tybalt.

I could tell he knew every word of what he was saying, and he was speaking crisply, clearly and unlike a lot of new actors, he wasn't going too fast.

Good job, dude, I thought. *You get it.*

But Edmund—Benvolio—was something none of us had seen before in that theater. Something I'd never seen before anywhere. From the time he asked "What is this Tybalt?" it was like Drew and Bobby were ghosts.

I mean, I couldn't take my eyes off him. None of us could. He almost danced on the balls of his feet. He threw back his head when he spoke. His voice was like a bell ringing against the ceiling and flying out into the darkness. He was smooth as satin and dangerous as a panther. I felt a sneaky damn glow coming into my heart.

They ran the scene up to the place where Juliet's nurse enters. Today, Gillinger didn't read her in. He didn't say "Thank you," either, the way he always did when actors came to the end of their scenes. Instead, he made Edmund, Bobby, and Drew stand there while he rustled some papers.

Finally, out of the dark came a single barking "Hah!" and he said, "Same scene. Jenkins, read Mercutio again. Ruspoli, read Benvolio. Shakeshaft, read Romeo."

And they did. And when they were done, Edmund was Romeo and Bobby wasn't. Everybody in the theater knew it.

The tryouts went on. Gillinger paired different actors, had them swap parts, just like he'd done with Edmund, Bobby and Drew. It was all just the way any tryout is supposed to go. But there was something different in the way Gillinger was acting now. He was interested in what he was doing.

Last of all, he put Edmund together with the potential Juliets, doing the balcony scene. And every one of us was thinking, "O, that I were a glove upon that hand that I might touch thy cheek," or words to that effect.

Gillinger read all of us, then five of us, then three, then two. And those two were Vivian Brandstedt and me.

I have to say, Vivian put everything she had into it, or everything she could with her clothes on. But Edmund threw her off. She was used to being the one giving the hots, not the one getting them. She even blew some lines. It gave me hope.

When I got up on stage with Edmund, I felt like I was

stepping into an enchanted place. What was real, what was pretend? I was falling for Edmund. Was he falling for me? Then I realized what the enchantment was made of. There was no real, no pretend at this moment. It was all one thing. One thing I could inhabit with everything I was right at that moment.

I let my new, nervous feelings take me into the role, and I played Juliet, and I was Juliet, for a few fantastic minutes. And Edmund was my Romeo. Oh, yes, he was.

When he said, "But soft! What light through yonder window breaks? It is the east, and Juliet is the sun," he sounded different than he had with any of the other girls. There was a little catch in his voice, a hesitation that said, *I'm not good enough for her.*

It gave me a pang, and I wanted to give him something to say, "Don't worry about it, I'm yours." But I couldn't. Juliet doesn't know he's there. And she's feeling the same misery he is. So I took the pang and folded it into the feeling I had to show, and I said "Ay me." And the way it came out of me was perfect, so full of longing you'd know she was ay-me-ing about a boy if you'd missed every word of the first three scenes of act one.

And it only got better from there. Gillinger read the Nurse's lines, and we took the scene as far as Bobby had taken it with Vivian the day before. And he and I were working together, building that scene second by second and word by word into something true and fantastic all at once, and I felt so proud of us that when we finished, and some of the people in the auditorium applauded, I wasn't even surprised.

"Thank you," Gillinger said. "You may sit down."

Chapter Eight

He kept us all waiting while he shuffled some papers again. Finally he stood up and walked on stage.

"Well," he said. "I'm glad that some of you went out and scoured your various 'hoods for bodies. I begin to think we may be able to cast this thing after all. My choices will be posted tomorrow afternoon, on the door to my office. If you are not a student of mine, you will receive a call tomorrow evening, *if* you have been cast. If you do not receive a call from me, you may consider that you are at liberty to seek other opportunities. Thank you all for coming. Good luck."

I grabbed Edmund's hand. "You were hot," I told him.

"And ye were a revelation! Something rough, but that's to be expected. Ye have a magic way about ye, cuz. Truly."

"Oh," I said, glowing inside. "Thank—thee, cuz."

And then Vivian Brandstedt was on Edmund's other side, practically rubbing up against him. "I'm so glad you came today," she said. "I really hope we can work together."

"Aye, so do I," Edmund said.

Vivian laughed. "You are so cute. Your accent and everything. You're really English, right?"

"I am a Warwickshireman," Edmund said. "And ye, where are ye from?"

"I am from right here in Guadalupe," Vivian said. "But I plan on going to England as soon as I graduate."

Why wait? I thought. *There are planes every day.*

"Come on, cousin, we'd better get home," I said.

"Oh, he's your *cousin?*" Vivian said.

I could see she was mentally crossing me off the list of potential competition for the English guy.

"Not exactly," I said. "Not like in this country. It's a complex relationship."

"Aye, complex," Edmund agreed.

"Can I give you a lift?" Vivian asked.

"Edmund gets carsick."

But Edmund said, "I think I will be well, cousin. I did not puke when your mother drove me here. Thank ye, Vivian. We will take your lift, and gladly."

She grabbed his arm and giggled. "So cute."

Drew showed up, then. Exactly ten seconds too late to offer a ride. I wanted to kick him. "Great working with you," he said to Edmund.

"I thank ye, Drew, and ye, Bobby. I hope we may all clap parts and clasp hearts."

Bobby hung back. He nodded, but the look on his face wasn't friendly. He gave Drew a little tug, and they went off.

"Let's go," Vivian said, but before we could leave Gillinger came sliding over from his seat in the third row.

"Very interesting resumé, Shakeshaft," he said. "Stratford Grammar School. And the Lord Admiral's Men. You're probably not aware, of course, that the Lord Admiral's Men haven't staged a play since 1631."

"Ye're right, milord." Edmund grinned. "I was not aware of it."

"So where did you actually get the chops I saw just now?" Gillinger wanted to know.

"Chops? Oh, anywhere I could get a part," Edmund said. "Anywhere at all."

"I see.... Well, I may have something for you. But don't lie to me again. You're good, Shakeshaft, but don't try to show off. You can't impress me."

"But ye will permit me to try, I hope." Edmund flashed that lethal grin.

"We'll see," Gillinger said. "If I cast you, you'll have to work on that accent. It's too thick for the kinds of audiences we'll be getting here."

"I am master of a dozen accents—Cockney, Welsh, Border Scots, French and Italian are me best. What would ye have?"

Gillinger just "Mmph'd" and walked away.

"What did I say?" Edmund asked.

"He just thought you were trying to impress him again."

"Can you really do twelve accents?" Vivian asked.

"Well enough. Can ye really drive a car?"

"Well enough," she said, practically smirking. "Let me show you."

"I hight—call—shotgun," Edmund said.

The ride home took about twenty years. Vivian and Edmund blathered away in the front seat like a couple of sparrows. But underneath the chitchat she was coming on to him like sex was going out of style, and he was loving every second of it. I kept hoping he'd barf, but he didn't, the selfish pig.

When at long last Vivian dropped us in front of my house, she waved goodbye in a way that said, "Get over here." And

Edmund gave the same low bow he'd given me when he'd thought I was Helen of Troy.

"Careful, Edmund," I said. "She eats guys for breakfast."

"Should I pour milk on meself?" Edmund asked me, and grinned.

"I'm serious, Edmund. She's bad news. Girls aren't the way they were the last time you went out on a date or whatever you did in England. They're a lot tougher and meaner than anything I'll bet you're used to."

Edmund hugged me. "Oh, cuz, ye are so good to me. I know ye mean to keep me safe from harm. But a man cannot keep his heart in a golden box. 'Twas meant to be given away."

He released me, and I stood there fighting the urge to hug him back. "Just be careful."

"Ye will help me keep from going wrong," Edmund said.

If only.

"Come on," I said. "Let's eat."

That was a long night. We waited up for Mom, and she and Edmund talked about everything that had happened at tryouts. I put in here and there, but I wasn't really in the room with them. I was doing what I did best, obsessing. Even-numbered minutes I obsessed about being Juliet. Odd-numbered minutes I obsessed about Edmund and Vivian. I hardly noticed when, after an hour, Edmund and Mom decided they were hungry and made popcorn.

Next day, I headed over to Gillinger's office as soon as the two-thirty bell rang. There were a bunch of us crowding around the sheet Gillinger had just posted on his door.

I couldn't look. I stood there with my head down, scared and hopeful. But finally, I forced myself to start reading from the bottom. There was a string of names next to SERVANTS AND CITIZENS, and mine wasn't one of them.

Neither was Edmund's. But Vivian's was. With my heart rising, I read slowly up the page.

TYBALT—BOBBY RUSPOLI
MERCUTIO—DREW JENKINS
(And!) JULIET—MIRANDA HOBERMAN
(And, at the very top!) ROMEO—EDMUND SHAKESHAFT

Edmund would play Romeo. And I was Juliet! He'd get his phone call tonight, but I was going to be the one to tell him. Me, his Juliet. Oh, yes. Life was good. I was so happy, I felt dizzy.

I read it all again and noted the understudies: Bobby for Romeo, Vivan for Juliet—me! I sat down against the office wall.

"Whoa, Miri, you okay?" Drew asked, bending over me.

"Just happy," I said. "Just totally, completely without any holdbacks or footnotes, happy. It's a weird feeling."

"Speaking of weird, he gave me Mercutio," Drew said, joining me on the floor. "I hope Gillinger knows what he's doing."

"Stop whining." I laughed. "You read for the part."

"Like I told you, I can *read* for anything."

Bobby loomed over us.

"Tybalt," he said. He didn't even say the word *understudy.*

"You'll be great," Drew told him. "Like Edmund said, he makes the whole play happen."

"Mmm-hmm," Bobby said. "Whatever. Let's haul it."

Drew offered me a ride home, but I wanted to walk. I wanted my wonderful feeling all to myself for a while. So I went slowly away from the theater where I was going to be spending all of my free time for the next six weeks, plus four performances.

The sky was brighter, the air was softer, the shadows on the sidewalks were more vivid. I walked extra-slow and took a long way home so that Mom would get there first and I could walk in and see the question that would be on her face, and answer it with my smile and tell her that I was doing this role for the both of us.

I'm Juliet, I kept saying to myself. *I really am.*

But when I walked in, Mom was nowhere around. Neither was Edmund.

"Hey, guys?" I called.

My answer was a horrible retching sound from the bathroom.

"In here," Mom said.

Edmund was curled up on the floor, and Mom was bending over him, looking worried.

"He was like this when I came home. He's been vomiting all day," Mom told me.

"I am so ashamed of meself," Edmund said. "I have not been thus—this—nervous about a part since I was fifteen."

"Oh, Edmund," I said, and knelt down by him, too. "You got it. You're Romeo. Bobby is Tybalt. And your understudy."

"Bobby is to be Tybalt, and understudy?" Edmund said. "Oh, God bless Bobby and make him the greatest Tybalt ever. And God bless Gillinger for making him play it. And God bless you, dearest cuz, for telling me. I think I will try to stand."

Mom and I helped him get to his feet. He wavered, grabbed Mom's shoulder, and staggered out into the hall.

"Bobby is to be Tybalt! Bobby is to be Tybalt! Oh, that is grand."

Mom and I followed him down the hall to the living room, where he sank onto the sofa.

"And Drew is Mercutio," I added.

"Aye. I mean, right," Edmund said. "But tell me, cuz, are you Juliet?"

"Yes! I am!"

Mom screamed and hugged me. Edmund pushed himself up and hugged us both.

"'Tis a consummation devoutly to be wished. Oh, cuz, I prayed we may work together."

The three of us sat around and waited for the phone to ring. I told Mom and Edmund every bit of trivia I could think of, then they asked me, and I told them again, slightly differently. Then Mom made tea for herself and me, and beef broth for Edmund.

Then we just waited.

And at five minutes after seven, the phone rang.

"Gillinger here," the voice on the other end said. "May I speak to Mister Shakeshaft, please?"

"It's for thee," I said, handing the phone to Edmund.

Mom and I watched his face while Gillinger spoke to him. It was like the sun coming up.

"Yes, yes. I would be very willing to play the role, sir. I—I am in your debt, sir. Tomorrow, aye. I will not fail ye, sir."

Edmund handed the phone back to me. He stretched his arms as far over his head as they would go. Then he rubbed his stomach.

"All's well that ends well," he said. "May we not eat? For I am rare hungry."

So there it was. I was Juliet. Edmund was Romeo. It looked like the spell I'd cast was working.

But a thought about the off-kilter spell kept entering my head as we ate: was there enough magic in it to make me Edmund's Juliet forever?

Chapter Nine

There were twenty-two of us in the classroom the next day. There could have been forty, but Gillinger had doubled and tripled a lot of the smaller parts. Besides me, Edmund, Drew and Bobby, all of the kids' parts were cast with students. But Romeo and Juliet's parents, the Chorus, the Prince, Friar Lawrence, the Nurse, and some other parts were being played by adults.

We were sitting around some pushed-together tables with our scripts ready and Gillinger at our head. Not only at our head, but sitting on a throne. The throne had been made for a production of *Once Upon a Mattress* back in the nineties, and Gillinger had been using it as his director's chair ever since.

"It's usual at the first read-through for the director to give the cast some idea of how he sees the play," he said. "But you've all been to rehearsals and you know how I see it. I see it as a burden that must be borne. If *Romeo and Juliet* proves anything, it proves that Shakespeare's reputation is based, at least in part, on crap. I know, he hadn't been writing very long when he wrote it. The play was written in 1594 or '95—"

"Ninety-three," Edmund muttered to me. "Winter of ninety-three."

"But I don't think that excuses him. The play is supposedly a tragedy, but structurally it's a comedy. Nothing that happens in the last two acts would happen if a couple of letters had been delivered when they were supposed to be. Everybody running around, missing each other. Give this play four doors and it would be a French farce."

Gillinger shrugged.

"Frankly, it reads like Shakespeare got to a certain point and couldn't figure out what to do next. The second half of this thing might as well be called *The Comedy of Errors II.* Except that a couple of overexcitable teenagers end up dead. But, we have managed to assemble a cast that I believe can take this Elizabethan turd and put a decent polish on it. Of course, a polished turd is still a turd. Nonetheless, let's begin. Act one, scene one."

And he pointed a finger at Bill Meisinger, who was Chorus.

Bill Meisinger was a fat middle-age guy with thin, greasy hair, but he had a beautiful voice. I'd heard he'd done radio commercials a few times. It was probably true, because that's just how he read his lines.

"*Two* households, *both* alike in dignity
In *fair* Verona where we *lay* our scene
From ancient grudge break to new mutiny—"

I could just see the two households: a couple of ranch houses in a really nice development. Something like 1593 Capulet Drive and 1593 Montague Court. But he did have a warm voice.

We whipped through the reading in a little under two hours. By the time it was over, everyone who hadn't already seen Edmund at tryouts was as blown away as the rest of us. It was like his reading had picked us up and carried us along with it. Everyone felt good about him, and about themselves, everyone except Vivian, who was pretty clearly not happy about being cast as a Citizen, a Gentlewoman and a Masker and nothing else, and Bobby was still mad. My—Juliet's—parents were Doris Lawson, whose voice was so soft I was afraid I wouldn't be able to hear her onstage (I wondered how the audience would) and Bill London, who had done a lot of community theater. He read with a very bad British accent. Romeo's father, Old Montague, was Jimmy Mahoney, who had been my eighth-grade science teacher. Lady Montague was Vivian's mother, Maria. She was a stunning, strong-looking German blonde. She read her lines like they were orders, and Bill played his like they were jokes.

Juliet has a nurse who raised her from a baby and can't stop talking about it. She was played by Ann Millard, who had a real British accent and read every line as if she expected to get a laugh.

But the most important adult role in the play is Friar Lawrence. He's Romeo's spiritual advisor, and an herbalist. He's the one Romeo and Juliet will both go to for help when they're in trouble. Sort of like a guidance counselor who deals drugs on the side. And that part was played by Phil Hormel.

He was thirty-something, a tall blond guy with no chin, who turned up in all kinds of plays in Guadalupe and the towns around. He claimed to have been a Broadway chorus boy, and liked to begin conversations with lines like, "You know, when I was in *Cats*—" but he had a gut on him that could have been cast in a show all by itself, so his dancing days, if they'd ever been, were long behind him.

He wasn't a bad actor, but he wasn't nearly as good as he thought he was. In fact, besides Hormel, there was only one person who seemed to think he was brilliant. That was Gillinger. They never missed a chance to work together.

It was just a little after nine when we broke up, and everyone who didn't already know Edmund came over to introduce themselves and tell him what a great job he'd done.

Drew put his hand on Edmund's shoulder. "Coffee?"

"Aye, sure," Edmund said.

"Where are we going?" Vivian said, smiling.

"The bookstore, I fancy," Edmund said. "That's where the coffee is."

Vivian laughed. "Oh, Edmund, there are lots of coffee places. You don't have to go to a bookstore. Don't they have coffeehouses in England?"

"Sure. The bookstore," Drew repeated. "Follow us there, Vivian." And he edged in between her and Edmund and sort of eased us toward the door.

But Edmund said, "Friend Drew, I will ride with Vivian. Her car, I think, will be more easeful to me. And I call shotgun."

"Great," Vivian said, and practically threw Edmund over her shoulder.

"See you in fifteen," Drew said. Then to me and Bobby he said, "Shall we go?"

Fifteen minutes later, we were standing in line at the bookstore café, waiting for Edmund and Vivian to show up.

"An interesting rehearsal, I thought," Drew said.

Bobby shrugged and fluttered one hand. "Just a read-through. Not a rehearsal. The real work starts now."

"Edmund certainly was impressive," Drew continued. "Has he played much Shakespeare?"

"I think so," I said.

"I heard a rumor that he played Juliet," Bobby said. "Is he gay?"

"Not hardly."

"Just asking," Bobby said.

"My good friend, I think you are feeling the gnawing bite of jealousy," Drew said.

"You know what you can bite," Bobby replied.

"Temper, temper. I'm here for you," Drew said and gave him a fake hug.

"I'm here for coffee," Bobby said, and ordered a mocha.

"Bobby has always harbored a strange affection for Vivian," Drew said. "Well, maybe not so strange. But affection, nonetheless. Or maybe not so much affection as unbridled lust."

"Like you don't," Bobby said. "Like any guy wouldn't."

"I admit the girl is stimulating—double espresso, please—but only until she opens her mouth. Then I feel my desire leaking away into the vast, empty caverns of her total vapidity."

I laughed. Good old Drew. If he could see what a ditz Vivian was, then Edmund would, too. He was probably figuring it out right now. All I had to do was give it a little time.

So why weren't the two of them here already?

"What are you having?" Drew said.

"Oh, nothing," I said.

"I'm buying."

"*Now* you tell me," Bobby said.

"Thanks, Drew," I said. "I'll have what you're having."

Double espresso. Not a good idea when you're already a little wired from waiting for a guy who isn't showing, I found out. After the third sip, I was so twitchy, Bobby said, "Calm down, Miri. He's fine. Viv's a good driver."

"*I am* calm," I almost yelped.

"I fear Vivian may have taken our leading man on a long detour." Drew smiled. "As she said, there are so many places to get coffee."

Bobby snickered.

"Oh, ha-ha," I said.

"I never knew you had such a hate on for Vivian," Bobby said. "What's up with that?"

"Nothing. I don't hate her. But—he's my cousin, you know?"

"On which side?" Drew asked.

"My father's…"

"The German Jewish side?" Drew said. "How does that work, if it's any of my business?"

"I mean, my mother's," I said. "That's the Brit side. Anyway, how did you know my dad's Jewish?"

"I heard you mention it once," Drew said.

"Huh? When?"

"Long time ago." And with that, he tipped his cup back.

That was funny. Before this week, I hadn't talked to Drew more than a dozen times, except to say hi. When would we ever have gotten onto the subject of my family?

"When did we—" I began, but Drew interrupted me.

"I don't remember. Just something you told me once."

"Whatever," I said.

"Listen," Drew said. "Let's have a deep intellectual conversation about our parts and why Shakespeare wrote this thing the way he did. I'll start."

"Screw that," Bobby said, and pulled out a deck of cards. "Let's play thirty-one."

So we played thirty-one. Three hands, then four. And I won every one of them.

But where was Edmund?

"I don't suppose either of you have Vivian's cell-phone number, have you?" I asked as Bobby was shuffling the next hand.

"If I had Vivian's cell-phone number, I'd be a much happier guy," Bobby said.

"What about Edmund's phone?" Drew said. "Or is he technologically challenged in that way, too?"

At that point, Edmund and Vivian came around the corner of the coffee bar.

"Sorry we're late," Vivian sang in a phony voice.

"'Twas a wrong turn we took, so deep in talk were we. But d'ye know, cuz, I think I could learn to drive a car, as ye said. Vivian does it right well, and she is no older than I. 'Tis all a matter of pedals and wheel, I believe."

"So cute," Vivian said. "Like you've never heard of driving."

In a coffee place, you're supposed to buy coffee. I had two dollars with me, which I shoved into Edmund's hand. "Go get yourself something."

"Oh, let me," said Vivian. "What are you having, Edmund?"

"I will drink whatever ye think best, Vivian," Edmund said. "And the next time we drink coffee, 'tis I will buy it."

When Vivian got back, she sat down between me and Edmund and said, "Let's get back to you driving, Edmund. Doesn't your family in England have a car? I thought everybody over there did."

"Not everybody," Edmund said. "Some of us—" He stopped.

"Anyway, I'd love to give you some lessons," Vivian said.

"So are we gonna talk, or are we gonna play thirty-one?" Bobby said.

"Thirty-one," I said. "Hit me, Bobby."

Playing cards, I was almost certain, was something that Edmund must know something about. And he did. In fact, he learned the game in about two minutes and then he won the hand. Plus, Vivian hated card games and had to pretend she didn't. Nice.

But it got late, and we had to break it up.

Vivian gave us a ride home.

We tiptoed in just after midnight. Mom had left a light burning in the living room when she went to bed. I got ready for bed, but I was awake. Wide awake. The espresso, no doubt.

I got up and opened my door when I heard Edmund coming down the hall.

"Hi, Edmund."

"Ah, cuz. Did I wake ye—you? I am sorry if so."

He came into my room and sat down in the chair by my desk.

"She is a strange creature," Edmund said. "I've never met her like in England. She is like your kitchen. Familiar in some ways and a world different in others. I know not how to take her."

"Do you know what a piranha fish is?"

"No," Edmund said and cocked his head to the side in curiosity.

"Then I don't have anything to compare her to."

"She talked most earnestly."

I wasn't sure how much more I wanted to know.

"She opened her heart to me," he went on. "She is most distressed that she is not Juliet. She told me how little Gillinger must value her to part her so small, and how hard she had worked for him in the past. She asked me if there were not some help I could give to make her shine even in her small roles. I told her I had had such parts, and always found something to do that made them worth the doing. She asked what I might suggest, and I told her a few things that might help. Then we came to the bookstore."

He pursed his lips. "There was one more thing."

I could feel my heart hit the floor.

"She kissed me. She said 'twas by way of thank you. But 'twas a long kiss." Edmund looked up at me. "How ought I to take such a thing, cuz? In England it would mean much."

I didn't answer.

"One moment she is almost weeping, as a girl would. The next, she is as a friend, or much the same as one. The next, she is a woman in my arms."

"An underage woman," I said. "Just remember, Edmund, this ain't England. She's under eighteen and you could end up in a lot of trouble with her if you're not careful."

"Even so?" Edmund said.

"Yeah, even so. Very big even so. *Huge* even so. Don't even think about it." I hadn't realized until after how much I'd been raising my voice.

Jeez, I was going over the top. Vivian was Vivian. She hadn't had the entire football team, but you could have put together a pretty good offensive line with some of the guys she had hooked up with. And by school standards she wasn't even a tramp.

"I will be wary," Edmund said. Then he sighed heavily. "When a man is taken by the fairies and brought to live in their world, he does not know the laws of the place. He may come to great harm ere he learns them, 'tis said. Good night, dearest cuz."

He got up and went to the door.

"Edmund," I said.

"Aye?"

"I'm glad you're here. Real glad."

He smiled and went out, and left me alone on my balcony.

Chapter Ten

"I must get money. A man cannot sit about all day doing nothing but waiting for rehearsals," Edmund said next morning at breakfast. "I want to make myself serviceable. And I want to help earn my keep."

"Edmund, you can't just go out and get a job here," Mom said. "You've got to have ID. Besides, you're under eighteen. That means there's a lot of restrictions on what you can do. But you're right. You need to be useful. Miri and I will come up with a list of skills you're going to need."

"But what of today?" Edmund said.

"Today is Friday," Mom said. "I've got to work and Miri's got school. Can we trust you not to get into too much trouble for one day?"

"Indeed I will not.... I can practice. That needs four hours a day. But whatever else ye would have me do, that ye will find me apt and ready for."

"Practice what?" I asked.

"Everything. Dancing, singing, juggling, fencing. And I must spend much of my time on Romeo. But a day's work is a man's duty. And he that doth it shall have the chinks." He grinned and shook his fist as though he had money in it.

"You can really do all that stuff?" I asked.

"Any actor must be able to do such things. Else the part goes to one who can."

"How would you like to wash the dishes?" I said.

Edmund laughed. "D'ye expect me to keel and scry for ye, cuz?" he asked.

"What?"

"D'ye not know keel and scry? Our sister Joan Hart, a mighty woman, can scrub a pot—we do call it keeling—in such a way that when 'tis filled with water she can look into it and see visions. That is scrying. And her visions are always true. But no man in our family has the power."

"No problem," I said. "All you have to do is wash and dry."

Edmund's smile disappeared. "In England that is women's work."

"Welcome to the U.S.A.," Mom said. "Here ye shall learn the manage of the vacuum cleaner or die trying."

"Whatever that may be, that I will most willingly, milady," he replied spiritedly. "As I will learn anything that pride does not forbid."

"Edmund, you've dressed up like a girl and gone on stage," I said. "How manly is that?"

Mom laughed. "Score, Miri," she said. "On second thought, don't try to clean up. In fact, just don't touch anything until I get home. Okay? I don't want you electrocuting yourself or something."

"Okay," Edmund said. After he finished eating, he got up from the table, picked up three oranges and started to juggle them.

"Cute," Mom said.

"An actor must be the master of many crafts."

"Save dishwashing, of course," I said. "Edmund, I'll see you after school. Rehearsal's at seven."

But when I got home, Edmund was gone. The TV was sending its blank blue glare into the living room, the *Riverside Shakespeare* was on the coffee table, and there were a couple of new dirty dishes from Edmund's lunch, but the guy himself was nowhere.

I went through the house calling, "Edmund, Edmund." Then I went outside and checked the garage, and every corner of the yard, but there was no sign he'd been there.

"All right," I told myself. "He's just gone out for a walk or something. He'll be back any minute."

But he wasn't. Four o'clock came, and a few minutes after that, Mom walked through the door.

"Edmund's gone!" I told her.

I must have said it with a little more emphasis than I'd meant to, because her face turned pale and she said, "Gone? Back to his own time?"

I hadn't even thought of that. And it was a horrible thought.

"I don't know—he's just gone."

So Mom went all through the house, too, looking for anything I might have missed. And when she didn't find it, she sat down on the couch beside me and said, "It's all right. He's been cast as Romeo. He'll show up in time for rehearsal unless he's dead or back in fifteen-ninety-whatever."

I had a horrible gnawing in the pit of my stomach. Because what Mom said made all kinds of sense. Edmund wouldn't have been likely to go wandering off without me. He didn't have anywhere else to go. So the likeliest thing was that Doctor Dee had figured out how to retrieve him and taken him back to England and brother Will, and I'd never see him again. Or he could be dead.

Or worse, with Vivian.

But a little after five he came through the front door. He had three oranges in his hands, and a pink piece of paper sticking out of his shirt pocket.

"One thing I have learned today," he said as he shut the door. "The constables of this place are no whit better than the ones in London. The pox on all of them."

"Edmund, what happened?" I said, feeling my fear evaporate like dew.

"Did you get arrested?" Mom asked.

Edmund sat down beside us. "I went out to earn some money," he said. "I only wanted to make myself useful."

"What did you do?" I said.

"After the two of ye left, I practiced my arts as I said I would. Then I made myself some food. Then I tried to think how I might profitably spend the time until ye came home. I read in Will's book. A thing called *MacBeth*. Very poorly writ. This fellow MacBeth has a wife who speaks of children that never appear. And there's this character Banquo who—"

"Edmund, get on with it," Mom said.

"Then I tried to watch the television machine," Edmund said. "But I could get no farther than conjuring up the big blue screen. And then I could not even unconjure that. This made me angry. So simple a thing, and yet I could not do it. I thought, 'What use am I to Miri and the dear lady her mother if I cannot do even the simplest things for myself? I will be a burden to them all my days.' But then I thought, 'Wait. Have I not got skills that may seem wondrous here? Miri tells me that but few can do those things that any actor in London knows better than he knows his catechism. I will make myself a blessing to them this day.' And I took these oranges and crossed the bridge over the freeway, and I went and stood in front of the bookstore and spread a cloth before me, and began to juggle.

"And it went well enough. Near everyone who went in or out by that door gave me something. But I was not there above an hour when this most officious little fellow all dressed up in blue and patches came to me and told me I might not do so. I must have permission, he said, and sent me on my way. 'Tis a large place, so I went over to the pub called Falstaff's, and there I did even better. But once again this yapping little feist comes up and says I must be gone. 'This is an authentic English pub,' I say, 'And I am English, too. I do but make it more authentic. In London, many a man who can juggle for pennies does so, and the pub keeper brings him beer. Leave me be.' 'Twas then he said, 'Get lost, Shakespeare.' 'Shake*shaft*' I did say. 'Me name is Edmund Shakeshaft.' 'Whatever' says the varlet and gives me this."

Edmund handed Mom the pink slip of paper.

YOU HAVE BEEN WARNED
You have been found in violation of the laws covering Public Nuisance, Loitering, and/or ________. You are herewith informed to quit these premises and not return without proper authorization. Violation of this warning will result in the immediate summoning of sworn law enforcement, and citation under the relevant statutes.
MALPASO ROW SECURITY

Mom sighed with relief.

"Dang, Edmund you've been busted," I said, laughing.

Mom shook her head. "It's nothing, Edmund. This isn't a real ticket or anything. That guy wasn't even an actual cop—

I mean, constable. He was just some underpaid jerk in a bad uniform. But he was right. Here, you can't just sing or dance or juggle in public for money. You have to get a permit."

"Damn such nonsense!" Edmund said. "Is every petty this-and-that a master of the revels here? How is a man to support himself? Be that as it may, I should most like to give you what I did earn."

And he reached in his pocket and handed my mom some money. "Seventeen and thirty-five," he said. "'Tis but the promise of better, milady."

"Aw, Edmund," Mom said, and she leaned forward and kissed his cheek. "What are we going to do with you?"

"Profit by me, I hope."

"Edmund, you have to be careful," I said. "If that had been a real cop, he'd have wanted to ID you. And you don't have anything, not even a student body card. You could have gotten into real trouble."

"Miri's right," Mom said. "Without identification you're literally nobody. And with your accent, nobody's going to think for a minute that you're an American. Which would make you an illegal alien. We've got to do something about this. You need an identity."

"I don't take your meaning," Edmund said. "What is this thing I need so badly?"

Mom showed him her driver's license. "As long as you've got a little piece of laminated plastic with your name and picture on it, you're somebody. Without it, it can be very hard trying to prove you exist, in the legal sense. Then there's a Social Security card, California ID—oh, my God, what about a birth certificate?" Mom said, panicking herself.

"This is major, Edmund," I said. "From now on, please don't go anywhere unless you have one of us along. Otherwise, those fairies'll get you for sure."

I could see Edmund wasn't happy with what he was being told. Trying to make my point, I said, "Bad fairies, Edmund. Very bad fairies."

He didn't smile, and my heart hurt for him.

"Edmund, I know this is a huge burden for you," Mom said. "No one else on earth has had to go through what you're going through right now. But plenty of people have come to this country from all over and learned to fit in. You will, too. You'll learn a little every day. In a year or less, you'll feel like you belong here, I promise. You do belong here. And Miri and I will help you every way we can."

"'Tis a wond'rous prison ye live in… I feel cabin'd, cribbed, confined, in spite of all your kindnesses."

Mom put her hand on top of his and gave him a sad smile. "You know, it's nearly dinner time. And seventeen thirty-five is just about the price of a great pizza. Edmund, it's time for your next lesson in Americana. Let's go."

Chapter Eleven

My mom should have been a doctor. She knew just what to prescribe. The Pizza Genius Giant Imperial Combo Feast cheered Edmund up, and he walked into rehearsal with me with a jaunt in his step.

The stage had been marked off with masking tape to show where parts of the set were going to be. And somebody had had the brilliant idea of using blue masking tape to mark off the Capulets' place and the pale yellow kind for the Montagues'.

"Get your masking tape right here," Drew said, coming up to us. "Blue for you, Juliet, and the other stuff for this guy. Wrap it around your arm."

"What's the idea?" I said.

"Gillinger wants us all to start bonding with our own side," Drew said.

"Hey, smart," I said, tearing off some blue tape and sticking it on my right arm.

"Too smart for Gillinger," Bobby said. "Drew gave him the idea."

"Oh, pshaw," Drew said.

"Well thought of, Drew," Edmund said, and practically covered his arm from shoulder to elbow with tape.

At seven, Gillinger called us all to order and we started the long, boring, absolutely important business of blocking the first act. Mostly this meant standing around waiting to be told to stand somewhere else. It felt a little like being back in kindergarten when you're so young you're still trying to learn how to line up. And it took a long time. Most of us, if we weren't wanted, stood outside talking, waiting for Tanya Blair to drag us back to the stage.

Not Edmund. He sat at the edge of the proscenium arch watching everything everyone did. And his big blue eyes didn't miss a thing.

And because I wanted to be with him, I sat there, too. At first, it was boring, except for being close enough to Edmund that I could feel the heat of his body and hear his slow, deep breathing. But as the night went on, I began to see the thing in front of us slowly coming to life. The life was in the changes that Gillinger made to his original ideas. They were small things, usually, but each one of them was like the twitch of a baby animal trying to stand up.

By the end of the evening, act one, the longest act, was about half blocked. That meant everything from the Chorus scene to just before the balcony scene. It's a huge chunk of the play and a lot of really dull work. But it was done, and it was also Friday night.

"Party. My place. Come on," Vivian whispered to Edmund and me as we were breaking up.

And before I could think of a good excuse why we couldn't go, Edmund was saying, "Silent as the tomb, swift as an arrow. See ye."

So we were going to a party. At Vivian's.

"I call shotgun," I said.

Oh, well, I thought. *What could happen at a party?* Knowing that the answer to that is, *everything.*

When we left the parking lot and headed toward Vivian's place, I was glad to see Drew's little 2CV tailing us.

"Have you seen Drew's car?" Vivian babbled. "It's so weird. Perfect for him, though. Know what he did in calc today? He told Mr. Kreps that numbers aren't reality. He said they just kind of open a window on it, like poetry. Know what's weirder? Mr. Kreps sort of agreed with him. Math and poetry. I mean, who but Drew? I'm afraid he'll end up in a rubber room if he goes on talking like that."

"But Drew is right," Edmund said. "I know not what a calc is, but I do know he was right. The lion stands for valor, the hive of bees for a well-run country. Fire for the passionate temper. These are simple things that everyone knows. But they are not so simple. For they all express the great truths that underlie everything else. And no matter how 'calc' a thing may become, still it must sing its part in the great song of being."

"That's so interesting," Vivian said. "I understand it now that you explain it."

"They are but common thoughts," Edmund said.

"Common? Excuse me, I don't think so," Vivian said. "Where did you go to school, anyway?"

"In Stratford. At the grammar school. But I was no hand as a scholar. My Latin was odious."

"Oh, my God, you know Latin?" Vivian squeaked. "That's unheard of. But grammar school. That's so cute. It must mean something different over there than it does here, right? Grammar school's for little kids. Nobody learns Latin."

Edmund had realized that he was starting to give too

much away. "Yes, it does.... But I couldn't tell ye—you—the difference."

I jumped in. "I like Drew's car," I said. "It looks weird but it makes complete sense if you know what's behind it. Did you know it's designed to carry a basket of eggs across a plowed field without cracking a shell?"

Vivian laughed. "That's probably why Drew bought it."

"Anyway, I'm glad you invited him."

"Oh, I didn't," Vivian said. "I invited Bobby. You invite Bobby, you get Drew. But it's all right. Drew's low-maintenance."

"Like his 2CV," I said.

"You see?" Edmund said from the back. "Drew is like his car and his car is like him. Everything is a metaphor for something else."

Vivian laughed. "So cute."

Chapter Twelve

Vivian's house had a pool, but it was too cold to go swimming. Or that's what I thought. But it turned out that Viv must have given some people enough heads-up time about tonight that they had suits with them. Bobby was in the water in a Speedo and a set of pecs that glistened like a pair of basking whales, and a couple of guys were batting a ball around with him, trying to act like seals. There were five or six girls in the kind of suits that get more expensive the smaller they are, and there was Vivian in her bikini.

Vivian in her bikini and Miri in her T-shirt and jeans. I had a pretty good idea why she hadn't mentioned this party to us earlier.

And Vivian in her bikini was a sight to behold. And Edward beheld. In fact, he couldn't stop beholding. I'd thought he was concentrating at rehearsal. That had been nothing compared to what he was doing now.

Please, Edmund's God, I thought. *Pneumonia. For Vivian. Please. Terminal pneumonia. Now, God, now.*

But before God could answer my prayers, Edmund dragged

me off to a corner of the yard where he could whisper to me and still keep his eyes on Vivian.

"Miri, do all girls disport themselves so?" he asked me. "Is it common to wear so little before the eyes of men?"

Damn it, Edmund, if I could get you to look at me like that, I'd wear nothing but a smile.

But what I said was, "Some of us, Edmund. But don't think too much of it. It doesn't mean anything. Especially to somebody like Viv."

"What does it mean?" he demanded.

It means you're an idiot, you idiot.

"I'd say it means she wants to go swimming."

"Would it be wrong for me to take off my shoes and get into the water with her?"

"Totally," I said. "Everybody would know why you were doing it and you'd be the biggest dork on the planet. Besides, your clothes would be soaked."

"How about if I were naked?" Edmund said.

"Worse. So worse. You know what's the best thing you can do now?"

"What? Tell me, faithful spirit," Edmund said.

"Turn your back. Walk into the house. Get into a conversation with somebody. Let her know you're in charge of your—let her know you're in charge."

"You are as wise as you are beautiful," Edmund laughed, and hugged me. I gasped, even though I knew it wasn't really me he was hugging.

"Did I hurt ye?" Edmund said.

"Don't be silly," I squeaked. "You just surprised me, that's all. Come on. Let's go find Drew."

The inside of the house was filling up. It looked like Vivian had just invited the high-school crowd. No Old Montague, no Friar Lawrence, no Lady Capulet and no Gillinger.

Still, we kids were most of the cast and the house was getting crowded.

Drew was in the kitchen, slicing some French bread into cubes.

"You aren't swimming tonight, friend Drew?" Edmund asked.

"Nay, friend. 'Tis the water. Cold. Nasty. Wet. I do concoct the spinach dip. Wilt try some?"

"'Tis thus we eat it," I said, picking up a cube and dipping it. "No muss, no fuss and very yum." Then I did one for Edmund and put it to his lips.

"So good," he said. "So yum."

My fingers tingled.

There was one member of the adult cast at the party. After all, it was her house. Maria Brandstedt came into the kitchen wearing a black bathing suit and a cougarish smile and helped herself to some spinach dip.

Maria Brandstedt looked the way her daughter would in thirty years, if she was lucky. She licked her fingers and asked Edmund how he liked America.

Edmund gulped and said, "'Tis like nothing I ever imagined."

"Well, we hope you like it here," Maria purred in her soft German accent. "I know Vivian is very glad to have you in the cast. So am I."

"As am I to be so."

"I understand you're a professional actor in England."

"I am a player, yes," Edmund said.

"Well, I'm really looking forward to doing this play," Maria said. "Come and meet my husband."

Dave Brandstedt was in the living room hanging out between the kids in his house and his liquor cabinet, which was in the same corner of the room as the baby grand piano. He had an empty glass in his hand.

"Hi," he said when he shook Edmund's hand. "Viv's been talking about you. Glad to have a face to place with the name."

"Give ye good evening, sir. Thank you for offering us this night of mirth."

Dave Brandstedt grunted. "You actors are always on, aren't you?"

"I do not take your meaning, sir," Edmund said.

"Rehearsal's over. You can talk the way you normally would," Mr. Brandstedt said. "In fact, I'd prefer it. I have a hard time with Maria and Viv doing plays. I don't mind the fact that they like to act. It's just that there are so many phonies in theater. Know what I mean?"

"Not precisely, sir," Edmund said. "What is a phony?"

"I think you know exactly what a phony is." Dave Brandstedt smiled.

"In truth, I do not."

"I'll spell it out for you," Dave Brandstedt said. "A phony is the kind of guy who memorizes somebody else's work and tries to pass himself off as some kind of an artist because he can remember it. The kind of guy who thinks he's God's gift to the world because he likes to pretend he's somebody he isn't. And a phony is the kind of guy who imagines he's got some kind of right to be treated better than everybody else. That's what a phony is. Got it?"

"Aye, sir. I will remember it."

"Excuse me. Maria, keep an eye on the liquor," Mr. Brandstedt said. And he went outside, probably to check out the high-school girls in their nothing-there swimsuits. Or to stand guard on his Venus Rising From the Sea daughter.

"Did I offend?" Edmund said. "How?"

"Edmund, I'm sorry," Maria said. "My husband's been drinking."

Edmund smiled and shrugged, and I tried to change the subject.

"How's your piano playing coming, Maria?" I said.

"Oh. So-so." She sighed. "I'm afraid I waited too long to ever be really good."

"I should like to hear ye play something," Edmund said.

I didn't see Drew come into the room with the spinach dip, but he was there now, standing beside me.

"How about you, Edmund?" he said. "Do you play?"

"Nay, I've never seen such an instrument," Edmund said.

"I can't believe that," Maria said.

"He means, this exact kind of piano," I said. "There's an upright in the house in Stratford. His sister plays. Right, Edmund?"

"Oh, aye. Right. Okay. But, as you say, cuz, it's an upright."

"Well, I do have a piece I'm almost good at," Maria said. "It's an old English thing, in fact. Maybe you know it."

Maria sat down at her piano, shuffled her music and opened *Greensleeves.*

"I do know this," Edmund said, and he sang as she played.

"Alas, my love, you do me wrong
To cast me off discourteously,
For I have loved you so long,
Delighting in your company.
Greensleeves was all my joy,
Greensleeves was my delight
Greensleeves was my heart of gold
And who but my lady Greensleeves?
Your vows you've broken like my heart

Oh, why did you enrapture me?
Now I remain in a world apart
But my heart remains in captivity."

It was amazing. Edmund had a voice like a violin on its way to becoming a trumpet. And he sang the song like he'd really lost the love of his life.

"That was wonderful," Maria said after they'd done all four verses. "Do you know any more?"

"Oh, a good many."

"Do one and I'll try to follow along."

"Here is one of my favorites," Edmund said.

"It was a lover and his lass
With a hey and a ho and hey-nonny-no
That o'er the green cornfield did pass
In springtime,
The only pretty ring time
When birds do sing
Hey-ding-a-ding-ding,
Sweet lovers love the spring.
Between the acres of the rye
This pretty country pair did lie
This carol they began that hour
How that love was but a flower
And therefore take the present time
With a hey and a ho
And a hey-nonny-no
For love is crownéd with the prime
In spring time
The only pretty ring time
When birds do sing
Hey ding-a-ding-ding
Sweet lovers love the spring."

Never mind how it looks on the page. You didn't hear it. I did. We did. And it was like listening to the sun shining through stained glass. I swear that song had colors that changed as you listened to it.

Maybe you had to be in love with Edmund to see the colors, I can't say. But I saw them, and I was. If I maybe hadn't been before, I was now. And it was like the world had shifted under me.

People began to drift in from the other parts of the house to listen. Mr. Brandstedt came back and leaned in a corner of the room, glaring. I saw his lips move. I couldn't hear what he was muttering, but it didn't look like a compliment.

"Sing something we know," someone said.

"I can only do a few songs properly," Edmund said. "All old ones like these, I fear."

"Oh, come on," the same somebody said. "You must know something modern."

"Even the Beatles," another somebody said. "Come on, Edmund, sing *Penny Lane* or something."

"It's enough for now," Edmund said. "Have we no spinach dip here?"

I grabbed the bowl and held it out to him.

"Dip!" I said.

Edmund scarfed up three pieces of bread at once so his mouth was stuffed. Smart guy.

"Where did you learn to sing like that?" Maria said.

"Imm Emmglunnd," Edmund explained, and reached for more bread.

And then Vivian was there, with her long wet hair framing her face and a bright red towel draped around her hips.

"Oh, Edmund, wow," she said. "Fantastic, dude." And she gave him a quick hug.

This time, it was Edmund who gasped, as much as you can gasp with a mouth full of spinach dip.

"Gotta go. Pool call," Vivian said, and twitched off back outside, leaving Edmund staring after her twitch.

"She's right. You're great, cuz," I said, wrapping myself around him the way she had.

But I had gone too far. Everybody could tell I was hugging him because Vivian had. The room was full of their thoughts: *Viv and Edmund. Miri and Edmund. Cat fight.*

"Line up over here to hug the English guy," Drew called out loudly. "Hug me while you wait."

"'Tis an honor I dream not of," said a girl who was in the party scene, and everybody laughed.

Pretty soon everybody was hugging Edmund, including the guys, and the whole mood changed. Now it was a joke.

Chapter Thirteen

The party was still going strong when Drew sidled up to me and said, "Listen, I have to work tomorrow. I'm taking off. If you want to leave now, I can give you a lift."

"Thanks," I said. "I'll try to detach Edmund from his groupies."

Edmund was out by the pool dazzling people with his juggling and his acrobatics and having the time of his life.

When I said, "Edmund, we have to go," there were groans, and a couple of girls wailed, "No! He can't."

But Edmund cartwheeled over to me, did a sweeping bow to everyone, turned back to me, and said, "Lead on, fair spirit."

There were the four of us. Drew and Bobby in front. We drove home with the canvas top pushed back and the wind blowing cool over us. Sea clouds had sailed in and covered the stars, and the night was a pale silver.

My hand wanted to reach out and take Edmund's and let Drew drive us on to forever under that sky. But the rest of me knew that wasn't going to happen. So I said, "I didn't know you had a job, Drew."

"Ten hours a week as a library page," he said back. "It's a good gig. Pay's not bad, and the hours are flexible. They're not scheduling me nights while I'm in the show. Otherwise, there's no way I'd have the time."

"What do you have to do?" I asked.

"Shelve books. That's most of it."

"It must be a wond'rous thing to be among so many," Edmund said.

"It's a skull-cracker," Drew said. "641.5932 White. 641.5932 Wilson. 641.5932 Yates. Half an hour of that and your brain wants to jump out and throw itself in front of a bus. But, yeah. I like it. Miri, you should bring Edmund down there and get him a library card."

"Oh. Yeah. Maybe."

I tried to shoot Edmund a warning look, but he missed it. He was sitting forward, asking Drew, "What is a library card, friend Drew?"

"Come on, Edmund. I know they have public libraries in England," Drew said.

"Of course we do. 'Tis this card I've never heard of."

"Give me a break," Drew said. "I work with an English librarian. She says it's just about the same there as here. You get a card and you check out books."

"Sure they have, Edmund," I said. "We'll go down and get you one tomorrow. Just like home."

"Great," Drew said. "Just bring your picture ID and anything with your current address on it. We'll do a card for you in five minutes."

"Ah. ID," Edmund said.

"Sure. Anything," Drew said.

"As soon as it gets here from England, we'll be down," I said.

"Just use your passport," Drew said.

"Me passport. Of course," Edmund said.

"Sure. That nice little document Queen Elizabeth passes out to her faithful subjects when they go to visit the colonies," Drew said.

"Elizabeth?" Edmund said. "You jest, friend Drew. Surely that old bitch is in her grave."

"What? When did that happen?" Drew said. "She was fine this morning. One of her weird relatives did something stupid and the paper was full of 'Her Majesty regrets exceedingly.'"

Edmund realized that Drew was not talking about the same Elizabeth he knew.

He sat back, silent. I was silent. Because what could I say that would make sense? And Drew was silent the rest of the way.

I was surprised when he swung by Bobby's house first. So was Bobby, I think. But he got out without saying anything more than "Later, dudes. Break it."

"See you tomorrow after work, dude," Drew said to him, and drove off.

Then we went slowly and silently back to my house.

When Drew pulled his car into our driveway, he turned off the engine. It was very quiet all of a sudden.

"Let me take a wild stab at something," Drew said. "Edmund isn't really English. Right?"

"*Wrong,*" I said.

"I'm as English as St. George himself!"

"That's kind of what I thought," Drew said. "St. George wasn't English, either, was he?" Then he said, "Look, I don't care. I like you, Edmund. Whatever you're covering up, I'm good with it. And I'm not asking you to tell me what's really going on. But if you want to tell me, maybe I can help."

No, no. This is bad, I thought. But I couldn't think of a way to turn Drew down that wouldn't make things worse.

Finally, Edmund asked, "What help can ye be more than you have already been, Drew?"

"What help do you need?"

"So much," Edmund said.

"Edmund, don't," I said. "Drew's a good guy, but if he knows, then Bobby's going to know. And if Bobby knows, sooner or later everybody will."

"Not true," Drew said, with a hint of annoyance. "I've been running interference for Edmund since he got here, and Bobby doesn't even realize it. And I'll go right on doing it, whether you tell me what's happening or not. I'm just saying, if I know what I'm helping to hide I can do a better job."

"I can trust Drew," Edmund said. "He's already proven that I can."

And that was true, I realized. Drew had been covering for Edmund tonight. And before, when Vivian was so interested in why Edmund didn't know how to drive. Maybe being a little weird himself made Drew able to pick up on weirdness in general. In any case, he'd figured out from the start that there was something strange about Edmund and that it needed to be protected. But still. But still.

"I will tell ye, Drew," Edmund said at last.

"You'd better come into the house, then." I sighed. "But 'tis an idea I like not."

Chapter Fourteen

It turned out that Drew had actually heard of Doctor Dee. Of course he had.

"He was the greatest polymath of the Elizabethan era," he said. "I think so, anyway. Better than Francis Bacon any day for my money. I mean, Dee would try anything."

"Aye, that he would," Edmund agreed. "Bacon's learning was but a flitch to Dee's."

Which made him and Drew snort, and made Mom and me look at each other.

"Flitch. It's a cut of bacon," Drew explained.

"Hilarious," I said.

"But how do you start out with necromancy and end up with time travel?" Drew said. "Wait. Maybe I sort of get it. Necromancy, raising the dead, may in fact be the suspension of linear time and its replacement by nonlinear time over a limited area defined by the pentagram. But no, because then—"

"Nonlinear time?" Edmund said. "Drew, ye make no sense."

"He means something like synchronicity," Mom said.

She had gotten up when we came in. She was sitting in Dad's armchair looking sleepy and beautiful in her gray kimono with the cranes on it.

And now it was Drew's and Edmund's turn to look blank along with me.

"Synchronicity is an important concept in Jungian psychology," Mom said. "What we call coincidence isn't at all. Things happen together but not because of cause and effect. We don't know why, but we know that they do."

"Mom, how did you—?" I began.

"I'm married to your father," she said and shrugged.

"And that sounds a lot like what we seem to see when we look at subatomic reality," Drew said. "I wonder if what Doctor Dee isn't—wasn't—isn't—whatever—transposing sub-atomic time and super-atomic time? In any case, my guess is that Edmund got caught in that channel. Doctor Dee opened it, Edmund fell into it and Miri, you pulled him out. Your spell formed the other end of the channel."

"But how?" I said.

"Maybe you touched synchronicity," Drew said.

"Drew, this is all very interesting, but it's not very helpful," Mom said. "Whatever happened, we have to deal with the results. Edmund's here. And we have to proceed on the assumption that he's here forever."

"Right. You'll need a birth certificate," Drew said. "One that says you're at least eighteen. Yeah, eighteen's perfect. You're old enough to be an adult, and too young for anyone to wonder why you haven't shown up on the radar screen before. Then there's voter registration, draft registration. Pretty soon we'll have you so nailed down in the twenty-first century you couldn't leave if you wanted to."

"But how can we get him a birth certificate?" I said.

"I'll work on it. And, Ms. Hoberman, do you still have an old cassette recorder?"

"Yes. Why?"

"We have some accent reduction tapes at the library," Drew said. "I'll check them out for you, Edmund."

"Farewell, Warwickshire. Edmund must sound a new note…." Edmund said. "And mayhap I can paint myself like a red Indian, too. What d'ye think?"

He smiled when he said it, but he looked so sad I wanted to hug him.

"Intriguing. But unnecessary," Drew said. "If you have any more great ideas like that, do share them, though."

"I will," Edmund said. "And Drew, if ye have any more thoughts about subatomic synchronicity or whatever it may be—"

"I'll let you know," Drew said. And he went out the door muttering, "Time travel...necromancy…metaphors for…?" or something like that.

"There goes a mighty mind," Edmund said.

"Nice kid," Mom said.

I was glad now that we'd let him in on Edmund's secret. Drew might have been a little weird, but so was the secret. And maybe a weird guy was just what Edmund needed now to help keep him safe.

The next afternoon, Drew was back.

"The accent tapes," he said. "Keep them as long as you need. I set them to 'Missing' in the computer. We'll search for them for six months, then they'll either magically reappear or be discarded."

"Whoa, Drew," I said. "Bandit, dude."

"No harm, no foul. They're tapes," Drew said. "They

haven't been checked out in three years. Who has a cassette player anymore?"

"Just this ancient, withered crone, apparently," Mom said as she walked into the room.

"I just meant it's—it's really okay—just this time—to do this," Drew stuttered.

"Thank ye, Drew," Edmund said. "I promise ye your generosity will not be wasted." He took one of the tapes out and turned it in his hand, trying to figure it out.

"There's one more thing. I hung around the library after my shift and did a little research in the newspaper back files. I found a guy named Kenny Kramer who died in a swimming accident about ten years ago. Local kid. Born at Bannerman, in fact. You apply for a birth certificate in his name, and you'll get it in a few weeks. I downloaded a hard copy. I thought you might feel more comfortable with that than doing it online."

He handed Edmund the application and a copy of an article that said *Local Swimmer Dies Tragically.*

"Drew, you're wonderful," Mom said. "Criminally inclined, perhaps, but wonderful."

Drew blushed. "Thanks."

Edmund rubbed his chin as he read the article. "'Tis just as we talked about," he said. "Yet I like it not. I cannot say why."

"Just do it," Drew said. "Once you're Kenny Kramer you can apply to change your name to anything you want."

"Right. Like Edmund Shakeshaft," I said. "Only the three of us ever have to know you were someone else for a little while."

"I don't see that you really have any choice, Edmund," Mom said. "And Kenny Kramer won't mind."

"I must be ruled by ye," Edmund said. "I know it. But for some reason my heart revolts."

"'Twill all be well," I told him. "Fill out the form."

And he did, in his jagged, loopy Elizabethan handwriting. All three of us volunteered to do it for him, but Edmund insisted on doing it himself.

"If 'twere done when 'twere done, then 'twere best done quickly," he said. "And by meself and no other."

When he was done, none too quickly it turned out, we put it in the mail to go out on Monday.

Edmund looked shaky. I put my hand on his arm.

Then he whipped around and clutched me to him.

"Oh, cuz, I know what 'tis. 'Tis goodbye to England. To all my old life and everyone in it."

Dad always said that when someone went through a big change they went through it over and over. That's because different parts of us learn at different rates. So, where Edmund had accepted the fact of his being stuck in the twenty-first century almost as soon as he'd understood it, applying to be one of us had reached a whole new level, and that level had to grieve.

Mom tried to put her arms around us both.

All three of us shook with his sobs.

After a while, Edmund let me go.

"Thank ye both," he said. "Excuse me now. I must be alone to pray, I think."

He went into his room.

We heard him start to cry again.

"Isn't there anything we can do?" I asked Mom.

"We're doing it, hon. They also serve who only stand and wait."

"Is that Shakespeare, too?"

"Milton. But it's true."

"I guess I'll go in my room, too," I said.

"All right," Mom said. "Damn it, I wish your father were here."

So I sat in my room and listened to Edmund crying, and cried for him. *Oh, Edmund, I'd do anything I could for you,* I thought. *You just have to ask.*

My tears fell onto the damp patches he'd left on my shirt, and they flowed together.

Chapter Fifteen

After I felt a little better—a little calmer, anyway—I went back out into the living room. Mom was sitting in her chair reading.

"Do you want dinner?" she asked.

"I want to *make* dinner."

"You do?" Mom said, and her eyebrows shot up. "Are you sure you're up for it?"

"Yeah. I'm tired of only standing and waiting. I want to do something."

"Then don't let me stand in your way keeping you waiting. What are we having?"

"I haven't got a clue," I said. "Maybe something English."

But I didn't know what they ate for dinner in London in 1597, and whatever it was, we probably didn't have it anyway. I ended up making a huge salad with chicken and toast croutons in it. Chopping all those vegetables gave me a good feeling.

We ate it, and then we did the dishes together and went back into the living room. Mom went back to her book, and

I tried to do my English assignment, but I couldn't pay attention to it. I read all the way to the end of *The Great Gatsby* and didn't even get that Gatsby died.

Then we went to bed, and I lay awake listening for Edmund. That was a long night. Milton had it right.

The next morning, Edmund came into the kitchen smiling.

"Give ye good morrow, fair ladies," he said, hugging us both. "And a fair, rare morning it is."

I was about as surprised as I'd have been if he'd come in wearing a suit of armor, a feather boa and a stuffed baby alligator on his head. More surprised, actually.

"You want some breakfast?" I said.

"I am near starved. A night on his knees can give a man an appetite!"

I got up and made him some bacon and eggs, feeling delighted that there was something I could do for him.

Edmund sat down beside Mom.

"So. You seem a lot better," Mom said.

"My courage came back with the dawn," he said. "Truly does the Bible tell us, 'A night of weeping bringeth joy in the morning.'"

"Uh-huh," my mom said. "You must be pretty tired, though."

"I do not feel so. I should, but I do not. Miri, may we not do some work together on our parts today?"

"Sure," I said. "Great."

Edmund wolfed his food while Mom finished her coffee.

I started humming. A day being Romeo and Juliet with Edmund was exactly what I wanted.

But Mom, with a little nod, clued me to follow her out to the front door. There, she whispered to me, "He's acting too cheerful. I think he may be having a huge mood swing. People do it under emotional pressure. Perfectly normal. Just don't be surprised if he crashes again, or does something a little desperate."

"Desperate like how?"

"You'll know it if you see it, I think," Mom said. "Call me if you need to. I'll be home after three."

She hugged me and left.

By the time I got back to the kitchen, Edmund already had our scripts out.

"Shall we start with the balcony?" he said.

That morning was intense. Edmund was on fire. He kept turning every word, reading both parts, reading the lines differently each time. Or sitting with his eyes closed while I read the lines, his and mine. It was like he was trying to make Juliet's moonlit garden real there in our kitchen.

After three hours of that, I needed to calm down, but not Edmund. He was all psyched about something, and unfortunately it wasn't love for Miranda Hoberman.

"I feel as if Romeo is truly opening up to me for the first time," he said. "Until this morning Dick Burbage's work has been in my mind, and my hope has been to equal him. But now I begin to see my way to make the part my own. I see things that Burbage could never see, because he never played Juliet, as I have. Oh, Miri, I feel power in me."

Power. That was the word for it, all right. Some strange energy was coursing through him, making him fly. Maybe it was Mom's mood swing going full blast. Or maybe he was a genius.

The phone rang.

"Hi, it's Drew," Drew's voice said. "Bobby and I want to work on our parts today. And I thought maybe you and Edmund would, too."

"That's funny," I said. "Edmund and I are working now. Why don't you ask him what he'd like to do?" and I handed over the phone. But I gave it to him backwards, accidentally. I wonder what Dad would have said about that.

We got the phone turned around, and Edmund held it like it was something live and squirmy.

"Ah, halloo?" he said into it. Then, "Aye, aye. 'Tis well thought of, dude. Aye, we shall be ready at twelve-thirty. Aye." He gave me back the phone and I smiled into it.

"Sounds like a date," I said, a lot more happily than I felt. I could have stayed on that balcony with Edmund all day. But, I told myself, it would be good for Edmund to have more rehearsal time with the guys. And I'd still be with him.

So I made us lunch and washed the dishes and right at twelve-thirty there was a knock on the door.

And it wasn't Drew.

It was Vivian. She was wearing a slinky black leotard and a wispy little rehearsal skirt and a big, phony smile.

"Hi, guys," she said. "Did Drew call back?"

I checked my phone. I'd had a call, but I'd turned my phone off without meaning to. Or, as Dad would have said, without my consciousness admitting to it.

And it had been Drew, calling to let me know that Bobby, damn him, had called Vivian and asked if she wanted to be in on what we were doing. And here she was to pick us up and take us over to Drew's place. Lovely. This day was getting better and better.

Plus, Edmund's eyes lit up like a wolf's when he saw her.

"It's so nice you can do this for me," Vivian said as they went out the door. "I want so much to be a good Juliet, even though I'll never get the chance to play her."

"'Tis only what one actor owes another," Edmund said.

Yeah, right, Edmund. You're only thinking about her performance, I thought, and ground my teeth.

The five of us sat around in Drew's living room, which was big and dark and furnished with tall green bookshelves and not much else except an old-fashioned sofa, and a line of wooden chairs that Drew had brought in from the kitchen table. The lowest row of bookshelves was wider than the others. They made a sort of bench that ran almost all the way around the room. There were a few big pillows stacked on the floor and in the corners of the shelves.

"Neat room," I said, taking in all the books.

"We call it the Book Forest," Drew said.

"'Tis like the Forest of Arden in *As You Like It,*" Edmund said.

"Like how?" I said.

"The Forest of Arden is no real forest," Edmund said. "'Tis a magical place where anything might happen. So is this forest, filled with the spirits of the trees from which the books were made and with the voices on the pages that whisper to the reader."

"So cute!" Vivian said.

"Well, let's see if we can do a little magic of our own," Drew said.

But it wasn't magic that happened in Drew's living room. It was drama. Only not the one Shakespeare wrote.

It was supposed to be the kind of rehearsal where you make suggestions to each other. Then the polite thing to do is try them and see how they work. We started with Bobby and Drew, and Edmund reading in the extra characters in their scenes.

The first time Edmund tried to give Bobby a pointer

about his reading, Bobby said, "Thanks," and went on doing what he was doing.

The second time, Bobby shrugged and ignored the suggestion.

The third time, he said, "Look, Ed. I know you've done the play. But when I want your help, I'll ask for it. Okay?"

"Your pardon," Edmund said, and stopped making suggestions.

After about half an hour, Edmund and Vivian took over. That was when things went from tense to gamey. Vivian wasn't even pretending not to come on to Edmund. And he wasn't even pretending not to notice.

She rolled her eyes at him. He strutted, if you can strut sitting down, and tossed his hair like some supermodel in a shampoo commercial. I mean, they were ridiculous. Disgusting.

I was furious. I was hurt. And I wasn't the only one. Bobby was looking at Edmund like he wanted to break his neck. And Vivian knew it and was playing up to Edmund even more.

Drew had said Bobby had a thing for Vivian. Apparently it was a big thing.

After a half hour of that, Drew said we ought to switch off, and suggested that he and Edmund do their scene where Drew makes fun of Romeo for being in love. But Bobby said, "I'd really like to work on the place in act one where Tybalt meets Romeo at the party. Drew, you can read Juliet's old man."

Drew agreed, and we went into that ill-fated in-your-face encounter.

Bobby put all his anger into that little scene, and Edmund played it as if it was the biggest joke since the last time Mercutio did standup at the Verona Comedy Club.

Neither of them were really acting the characters. They were just using them to tell how they felt about each other.

And Vivian was smiling this little cat smile.

I wanted to smack her.

Finally, when we were all nice and tense, Drew said, "There's stuff in the fridge. Let's take a break."

Because some of us need to cool down.

We were sitting around with sodas when Drew's mom came home. Ms. Jenkins was a tall, willowy woman with an ordinary face, except for her eyes which were glowing brown. There was something unusual about her, though. She was wearing beautiful green robes trimmed with gold lace, and a big silver cross around her neck.

"Everyone, I'd like you to meet my mother," Drew said. "Mom, this is everyone. Vivian Brandstedt, Edmund Shakeshaft and Miranda Hoberman."

"Hello, everyone," Ms. Jenkins said. "It's nice to meet you."

Edmund looked stunned.

"My mom's a priest," Drew explained. "How come you're still in uniform, Mom?"

"A parishioner's mother died today. At Bannerman. I gave the last rites," Ms. Jenkins said.

"Are you okay?" Drew asked.

"Yes, thanks. But it was very sad. Except for her daughter the poor woman had outlived everyone she knew."

"My mom fills in some Sundays at Episcopal churches," Drew explained.

"Episcopal churches?" Edmund said. "What may they be?"

"The American name for the Church of England," Ms. Jenkins said.

Edmund looked shocked. I could see he wanted to ask more, but he was afraid to. He didn't know what pianos there were in this room, and he didn't want to reveal that fact. But he stared after Drew's mom like she was a fairy, a monster, a ghost or all three. Or maybe even a demon. Drew saw it.

When she went out of the room to change, Drew said, "My mom's what's called a working priest. That means she has a day job. But sometimes she substitutes for clergy who have parishes. And she's on-call at Bannerman when somebody wants an Episcopal priest."

"What's her regular job?" I asked.

"She runs a yoga studio," Drew said.

Edmund shook his head. A woman priest was too much for him to handle. His concentration was gone. Something had shifted and we all felt it. The rehearsal, or whatever this was, was over.

"Well, thanks, everybody." Drew sighed. "I hope this helped. We'll see what tomorrow brings."

If tomorrow is anything like today, I thought, *what tomorrow brings won't be so good.*

But as it turned out, I didn't have to wait that long.

Chapter Sixteen

That night, after the three of us had eaten dinner and the dishes were done—without any assistance from any Englishmen, by the way—Edmund yawned and stretched and went to bed.

That bothered me. I wanted to get him all to myself and warn him away from Vivian. But, I told myself, he'd been up all last night. He needed the sleep. Mom and I watched television together and went to bed at our regular time.

I fell asleep worrying about Edmund.

Then, at three that morning, I jerked awake with my heart pounding like a jackhammer. Someone was sneaking into the house, climbing in through a window. I could hear it.

I reached for my phone to dial 911.

And I heard Mom say, "Edmund, what the hell?"

And Edmund said something like, "Milady, did I wake ye?"

I got up.

Edmund was standing in the hall in his day clothes and his shoes were wet and had bits of grass on them.

"The next time, come in through the door," Mom said.

"Aye, the window of me room is something too high," Edmund said, smiling like a naughty little kid. "'Tis easy enough to go out so—"

"You don't need to sneak out of here," Mom said. "Just tell us where you're going. Where were you, anyway?"

"Ah, I was ranging about a bit, milady. More than that I cannot say," Edmund said.

He didn't have to say. I knew exactly where he'd been. Vivian's perfume was hanging on him fresh as new paint and twice as tacky.

Mom sniffed it, too.

"Hmm. More than that you don't have to say," she said. Then she turned to me. "Miri, go to bed. I have some things to discuss with Edmund."

"I have some things to say to him, too," I said.

"Yours can wait until tomorrow. Mine are clinical."

I walked out into the living room and sat down.

"Miranda," Mom said.

"Mom."

"What?" Edmund said.

"Miranda, I want to talk privately with Edmund. Now."

"Mom, there is nothing you can tell him that I don't know about," I said. "And as far as Vivian goes, I know a lot more than either of you."

"I won't speak of Vivian—or anyone—to the pair of ye. A man, a proper man, would do no such thing."

Mom looked at me for a moment before continuing. "Do you at least know what a condom is?" she blurted out.

I blushed. Edmund didn't say anything. And Mom, she told him exactly what it was, how to use it and why he was a damned idiot if he didn't use them.

Edmund stood there with his arms crossed like he was too noble to know what she was talking about. The idiot.

And I sat there trying to look cool and cringing inside.

When Mom had finished her little lecture on twenty-first-century hygiene and the wonders of not getting girls pregnant, he turned to me, and said, "And ye, Miri. What would ye have me know?"

He looked as arrogant as Tybalt.

And I realized that I couldn't say anything. Because what I wanted to say was unsayable, especially in front of my mom. A lot of things about Wrong Girl Versus Right Girl.

"Well?" he said. "What do ye wish me to know?"

And like magic I knew what I could say.

"I've got just two words for you," I said. "Anne Hathaway."

And Tybalt vanished from Edmund's face.

"Ye, ye know about that?" he stuttered.

"I told you your brother was famous."

"But 'twas more than four hundred years ago…."

"Miri's right," Mom said. "Everybody who knows anything about Will Shakespeare knows he got Anne Hathaway pregnant and had to marry her."

"How'd that work out for them?" I asked.

"None so well," Edmund admitted.

"Okay, Miri. Do you have anything more you want to say?" Mom said.

I thought it over and shook my head.

"Then go back to bed while I tell Edmund a few more things. We won't be long."

I had to. Mom had cut me some slack, slack I mostly couldn't use. So I got up and went back down the hall, wishing I could come up with a really great parting shot. Which I couldn't.

I lay in bed wishing I'd had the foresight to bug our house so that I could know what Mom and Edmund were saying to each other right then. But Mom was telling the truth. It wasn't more than a few minutes before I heard them both passing by my door on the way to their own rooms.

I punched my pillow and wished it were Edmund's face. Then I punched it six times and wished it were Vivian's.

"Damn Shakepeares," I said.

The next morning, Mom and I got ready to go our ways while Edmund slept in.

We didn't speak. We danced around, doing our morning routines as if we were two stars orbiting each other.

While she was standing over the stove, Mom said, "Are you okay?"

"Hell, no," I said.

Mom sighed through her long, elegant nose. "Try to be patient with him," she said. "He feels adrift. He's trying to find something to connect to. Someone."

"He's got us."

Mom didn't answer me. But I knew she was not-saying "'Yes. But he doesn't want just us', and meaning, 'Honey, he doesn't want you.'"

Damn, I was mad at her. Angrier than I was at Edmund. I ate my breakfast in three bites and got out the door four minutes early so I didn't have to talk to her anymore.

I went through the day in a fire of rage. At least I didn't have to see Vivian. We didn't have any classes together. But Drew and I were in AP English last period.

I sat there tapping my foot while Drew explained to us this insight he'd had that the eyes of Doctor T.J. Eckleberg, which are part of an old sign in the dump in *The Great Gatsby,* are really a metaphor for the absence of God in the post-World War One era. All very interesting and so totally Drew that I wanted to smack him.

And I must have been pretty obvious about it, because when class was over, Drew caught up to me in the hall and asked what the matter was.

"Nothing," I snapped.

"Well, if it were anything, and I could help, you could let me know. Would a ride home help?"

"Sure." I said this not because I wanted a ride but because I wanted to convince Drew I was okay.

So Drew and I headed over to the parking lot, where Bobby was already leaning against the 2CV.

"Hey," he said.

"Dude," I agreed.

Drew started for my place. We inched out of the lot and into the clumps of cars that choked the streets around the school.

We crawled down to the stoplight while kids on foot passed us by going faster than we were. None of us talked.

Finally we reached the light. It turned red as soon as we got there, of course. When, after a couple of hours, it finally turned green, Drew started out into the intersection. And from the opposite direction came some guy turning right in front of us, flipping us off as he went by.

Drew slammed on his brakes, and we missed the other car by a few inches.

"Whoreson heir of a mongrel bitch!" I shouted. And I stood up in my seat and flipped him off while I added a few more thoughts I had about him.

Drew let out a long breath, said something in a low voice and finished crossing the intersection.

"Whoa, Miri," Bobby said. "Where'd you get that one? I never heard you talk like that before."

But I wasn't finished talking like that, and I went on screaming after the guy even though he was nowhere in sight.

Bobby started laughing.

Drew pulled over to the curb. "Hey, are you all right?"

"I'm just *perfect,*" I snapped.

Drew put his hand on my wrist and I pulled away.

"Sorry," he said.

Bobby leaned forward. "Wrong time of month?"

He sounded so damned smug, like he knew all about women from his vast experience of his Girls of the Week that it made me even madder. I lost it. I turned around in my seat and almost screamed into his face, "Edmund's screwing Vivian."

All of a sudden, Bobby didn't look so smug. He sat back. "Big whoop," he said.

"Yeah," I said, trying to sound like I didn't care, either, which was stupid. "I mean, how dumb is that? My stupid cousin comes over from England and immediately starts messing around with the understudy. I mean, I really thought he was smarter than that. But what really worries me is what happens if her dad finds out."

"My guess is her dad knows as much as he wants to," Drew said. "However much that is."

"What do you mean by that?" Bobby said.

"I mean our Vivian is not exactly a blossom born to blush unseen. And her old man knows that, but doesn't really want to know any more."

"Ed's still under eighteen, right?" Bobby said.

"Yes," I said.

"That's good, 'cause if he wasn't—"

"Our production could suddenly find itself without its leading man," Drew said. "Hmm."

Drew had said what Bobby was thinking. I was sure of it. Damn it, Miranda, why couldn't you have kept your mouth shut?

But it wouldn't have mattered. By tomorrow night at the latest everyone in the cast would know about Edmund and Vivian. It's always that way in theater. And Bobby would have been just as angry no matter how he found out. And he was furious, I could tell.

"Yeah," I said. "You're right, Drew. That's why I'm so damn mad. I mean, what is it about guys?"

The two guys with me didn't try to explain what it was about guys that made them guys.

Drew drove me the rest of the way home.

"See you tonight," he said.

I slammed the door of his car without answering.

Edmund was sitting in the living room with Mom's old cassette player on the coffee table, and the TV on blue screen.

"Truly, cuz, I thought ye might be happy for me," Edmund said when I walked in the door.

"Why would you think that?" I said. "I told you what kind of person she is."

"Well, 'tis all one. A man must do what a man must do."

"That is the stupidest thing I've ever heard you say. In fact, it's right up there with what my dad said when he left us to go find himself. Men. You haven't learned anything in four hundred years."

"Miri, if a man did not hearken to his heart, naught would ever happen in this world," Edmund said. "Suppose my brother had stayed at home in Stratford instead of running off to London to act and write his plays."

There was something in his voice that was pleading for me to understand.

I looked at Edmund sitting surrounded by strange things

he hadn't ever imagined could exist, trying so hard to comprehend where he was and what he had fallen into. And angry as I was with him, I realized I still loved him as much as I had before. Maybe more.

"I'm just worried about you, that's all," I said finally. "About you, and about the play. I'm your Juliet, damn it. I'm worried you'll do something stupid to mess up the production."

"And lose me chance of being Romeo? I'd sooner turn Spaniard!"

I still wanted to strangle him. Or throw myself into his arms. Either one. But there was nothing I could do. Whatever Edmund and Vivian had set in motion would just have to work itself out. I sighed a deep sigh. "It looks like you've been working on your new accent. Want to give me a sample?"

Edmund stood up and declaimed, "I'm sorry, Madeleine, but our relationship isn't working. I'm going back to Elizabeth. The new Dice-O-Matic chops, dices and purees anything in your kitchen in less time than it takes to make a cup of coffee. Only sixty-nine ninety-five from your Dice-O-Matic dealer. Ken, we have a low front moving in over the weekend that should bring us some morning clouds that will burn off by midday."

He bowed to me.

"What d'ye think, faithful spirit? Do I sound like a countryman of yours?"

Actually, he almost did. His o's were still too long for an American, and some of his m's had a b-sound behind them, but it was a pretty amazing change.

"Just don't forget your Warwickshire accent, my good fellow," I said. "I like it right well."

"I shall keep it always, then," Edmund said, and grinned.

"I shall sound American only among strangers and sheriffs and suchlike fellows."

And fortunately Mom came home then before I could say anything stupid. And in a few hours it was time to go to rehearsal.

Chapter Seventeen

Vivian was waiting for Edmund when we got there and peeled him away from me.

Well, I had to expect it. I wandered around the stage like I was running over my blocking in my mind.

Gillinger strode into rehearsal exactly five minutes late. He had the smug smile I'd only seen on him when he was running tryouts. What could that be about?

"I have news that will be of interest to some of the younger members of the troupe," he said. "I've just had a call from an old acquaintance at the Ashland Shakespeare Festival. They are initiating a new apprenticeship program for high-school students next season. Two apprentices, a boy and a girl, will be selected each quarter to work at the Festival as members of the acting company during the long vacation, whenever that is for the school involved. So if you go to one of those year-round schools you may be going in the dead of winter, or the uncertainties of spring, or the vagaries of an Ashland autumn. Since Steinbeck is still on the old school year, anyone from here would be going in the summer. Which means you will face much stiffer competition than you otherwise would.

"In any case, the apprenticeship is for two months, is tenable only by students sixteen to eighteen, and can only be earned by nomination by a member of the Festival staff. Which means that one or more of them will be dropping by our little production to see if there is any talent in it. I mention this only because it may make some of you work harder than you presently are, which I can assure you, you need to do. All right then—"

I raised my hand.

"Yes?" Gillinger said.

"Excuse me, Mr. Gillinger," I said. "Could you tell us something more about the apprenticeships? Would we be cast in plays?"

"Why, yes, Hoberman. I thought I'd made that clear. The apprenticeships will involve being cast in at least one production. There would be little point in an apprenticeship without it."

Oh, my God, Ashland. Next summer. I saw myself there—with Edmund, of course; Vivian was dead—walking onto the stages where Mom had stood more than twenty years before, and working with the actors of the I-5 Repertory Company. Maybe even with some of the same actors my mom had worked with. Could anything be better than that? Could anything I could do say "I love you, Mom" better? My heart clamped down on the thought of that apprenticeship and gripped it like a steel glove.

"Edmund. That's us. Next year. It has to be," I whispered.

But before Edmund could say anything, Gillinger was talking again.

"All right," Gillinger said to the cast. "Let's see how much you've managed to forget in two days. We're going to run act one from the top to where we stopped."

It was bad. Some of us acted like we hadn't cracked open our scripts since Friday. There were a lot of mistakes, and every mistake needed its do-overs. It was nearly an hour before Edmund had his first entrance.

Enter Edmund. Head down. Sad face. Dragging his feet. The picture of sorrow.

Benvolio, a nice guy named Joey Romero whose love of theater didn't translate into acting talent, said to him,

"Good morrow, cousin."

Edmund answered,

"Is the day so young?"

He sounded like he was groaning a velvet groan. I could see Joey turn toward it trying to respond with a feeling, not just a line.

Joey said,

"But new struck nine."

Edmund said,

"Ay me, sad hours seem long. Was that my father that went hence so fast?"

And he gestured offstage like he was hailing a cab. It was elegant, but too much.

Joey said,

"It was. What sadness lengthens Romeo's hours?"

Edmund sighed.

"Not having that which, having, makes them short."

Then he waved his arm around and touched his forehead. It was beautiful, but it was corny.

Phil Hormel laughed.

Vivian giggled.

The scene went on, with Edmund's beautiful voice flowing like dark water and his body dancing a sort of over-the-top ballet. What was he doing? For a second I didn't believe Edmund had ever acted before. But I couldn't quite, because as stupid as what he was doing looked, he did it so well.

Gillinger let Edmund go on the way he was going until just before the end of the scene. Then he stood up. "Shakeshaft, what *are* you doing?"

"I am entering the scene," Edmund said. "I am impersonating sorrow."

"Don't impersonate anything. Don't try to act. It's only blocking. Just read the lines. And for God's sake, don't ever act that way again. You'll get laughed off the stage."

"I will? Why?"

"Because you're ridiculous," Gillinger snapped. "And I will not have a ridiculous production. You're carrying on like the worst kind of regional theater ham. Now for God's sake, just read your lines and walk through your blocking and don't try to *act*. And especially don't act in that phony fake Elizabethan style again. I've seen grade school kids do it better. Jesus."

That really threw Edmund off. He went through the rest of the scene speaking in monotones, hardly holding his head up. He almost stumbled once or twice when Gillinger told him where he wanted him to move. When it was over, he came back and sat down beside me, but he didn't really know I was there. He had turned his laserlike concentration on the play.

There was one more scene before my first entrance. It's an easy scene to block, with only two characters who are both sitting down, but the two scenes before it, which include the first sword fight and fill up the first half of act one, had taken almost two hours.

"Break!" Tanya called. "Fifteen minutes, everybody."

As soon as she said it, Edmund grabbed my wrist and jerked his head toward the wings.

I followed him into the darkness.

There, with the fly ropes hanging over our heads, and the smell of dust all around us, he whispered, "Miri, what did I do wrong? I swear I did nothing out there that Burbage himself would not have done. 'Tis where I got most of the business. What does Gillinger want of me?"

"It's okay, Edmund," I said. "You were just overacting. Tone it down and everything'll be fine." I took his hand and squeezed it. "You'll be fine."

"Tone it down? D'ye mean, pull into myself like a Puritan at his prayers? What kind of acting is this? How are the people at the back of the theater to know what we are doing?" Edmund looked scared and angry.

"Just be more naturalistic," I said. "I know it's different, but you can do it."

"*Naturalistic,* is it?" he repeated. "And what is that?"

I thought of something Gillinger had told us in class last year.

"Edmund, pretend there's a fourth wall between you and the audience. They can see us, but we can't see them. Then just act the way you would if you were really in that situation. What would you say to Benvolio if you didn't know people were watching you say it? How would you act? That's the whole secret."

"Act as if the audience is not there," Edmund said. "Who thought of that?"

"I don't know," I said. "But that's the way we do it. It's called the fourth-wall convention. What you're doing is too artificial."

"Artificial?" Edmund said. "What could be more artificial than pretending there's an invisible wall between us and the persons who've paid to see us? A wall in the middle of a street, forsooth. 'Tis nonsense. The audience *is* there. 'Tis true, they have come to forget, for a little, that they are so. 'Tis our task to transport them to Verona while they stand or sit crowded hip and shoulder together, and make them see fine houses, a moonlit garden, a monk's cell. But how can we do that if we do not *act?*"

"It's what Gillinger calls a stage convention," I said.

Edmund threw his hands up. "Of course it is. All acting is 'stage convention' as you call it. 'Tis all craft and artifice. What could be less natural than to pretend otherwise?"

"Edmund, calm down! It's just the style now. Something new to learn. That's all. You've dealt with all the rest of the world's changes pretty well so far. This is just another small one."

Edmund sighed. "Very well. I will convene. Now where is this wall supposed to be?"

"The edge of the stage," I said.

Edmund walked down to the footlights. I followed.

"'Tis not a stage, but a cage," he said quietly to me. "But I will learn to live in it."

And then, like lint on a black skirt, there was Vivian. "Hey, Eddie, you okay? Gillinger was pretty rough on you."

"Oh, 'twas—it was—nothing," Edmund said. "I did not understand about the fourth wall. Now I do."

"Gee, I thought everybody knew about the fourth wall," Vivian said. "Don't they have that in England?"

"It's all one. Gillinger has much to teach me," Edmund said.

"That's really brave of you to say," Vivian said, and gave him a dazzling smile.

"Oh, I am a very fox for valor," Edmund said, and gave her a sad little ironic grin that should have been for me.

"He's so cute," Vivian said directly to me. She put her hand on his arm, the one with the tape on it. "So *cute!*"

Grrrrrrr.

Tanya Blair was rounding everyone up. Break was over.

"If you're not in this scene, clear the stage," Gillinger demanded.

I was up.

Juliet's mother and the nurse have been talking about her for what seems like a very long time before she finally comes on. Then they spring a little surprise on her: Count Paris, this guy she doesn't even know, has asked her father if he can marry her, and he's said yes. Her mom's good with it, and the nurse is throwing out all this daffy stuff about how cute Juliet was when she was a baby, as if that had anything to do with anything, and I walk in on all this.

"'Tis an honour I dream not of," is what Juliet says when they tell her. I said it the way I thought it should be said. Surprised.

"Try that again, Hoberman," Gillinger said. "Think. This is your first entrance. With Shakespeare, that's always significant. It's our first look at the character. Your first chance to define yourself for the audience. Now, you're a thirteen-year-old girl who's just been told she's getting married to some guy she doesn't know. Give us some depth, for God's sake."

So I came in again, and this time when they told me, I said,

"'Tis an honour I dream not of."

Like I was scared to death.

"Better," Gillinger said.

But Edmund said, "I beg your pardon, Mister Gillinger, but I believe Miri had it right. After all, Juliet's but thirteen, but, as our poet says, girls so young are often wed in Verona. 'Tis not as if she had no idea such a thing could happen to her. It's a joyful thing to her as much as an unexpected one."

Gillinger turned around on his throne. He stared at Edmund for a long moment. Then he said, "Shakeshaft, you claim to be a professional. Act like one."

"How do you mean, sir?" Edmund said, giving Gillinger look for look.

"I mean, *shut up.* I'm directing this show, not you. I know things are different in the British theater. The director isn't as important there. Well, you're in the colonies, now, *sire,* and if I say she comes in naked on a Shetland pony, then that's how she's going to do her first entrance. If I tell you to stuff bananas in your ears, and paint your face blue, then that's the way it's going to be. Got it?"

"I understand. You do not want us to try to help you to a better play."

"You can help me by doing what you're damned well told."

Edmund hesitated, then bowed. "Milord," he said.

"Now, could we possibly continue with the first act?" Gillinger said, looking around.

And we did. And I did my first line Gillinger's way. And all my lines after that.

And actor by actor, Gillinger told us why what we were doing was wrong. We never finished the first act that night. We got as far as the beginning of the balcony scene and had to quit. It was after eleven o'clock.

We all left quietly, which was funny. Usually at the end of a rehearsal people got louder, letting off steam, shouting good-nights and setting up plans to get together. But the fight between Gillinger and Edmund had set everyone on edge. It was like being in Verona, everyone waiting for the next brawl to break out between the Capulets and Montagues and hoping that nobody would get killed. Edmund's ironic bow had ended the fight with Gillinger. But everyone knew it wasn't really over. And nobody could figure out why it had happened at all.

Except, of course, Drew.

"What's up with Gillinger?" I said as the four of us drove home in Drew's little car. "Has he been taking ego steroids?"

"Verily," Drew said. "That line about coming in naked on a Shetland pony was a bit much, methinks."

"So what's up with that?" I said.

"Perhaps he felt threatened," Drew said.

"Threatened?" I said. "Why?"

"Maybe he feels challenged by Edmund."

"I did not mean to offer him challenge," Edmund protested.

"That just makes it worse," Drew said.

"I get it," I said. "Cuz, here is the real thing."

"Yep. Our Gillinger is a wannabe big-time director. Being stuck here in Guadalupe gives him a stage to play the role of unappreciated artist. But in Edmund he senses something unpleasant. Someone that he suspects knows more about acting, and about Elizabethan theater, than he does. Worst of all, he senses a real artist."

"And so..." I said. I left it unfinished. There were too many unpleasant possibilities.

"Like a dog pissing on a rock to show the world he owns it," Edmund said.

I laughed suddenly.

"Concisely put," Drew said. "And guess who the biggest rock is?"

"What must I do, d'ye think?" Edmund asked.

"I don't think there's a good answer," Drew said.

"Wonder if Gillinger wishes he'd cast me yet?" Bobby said.

I realized it was the first time Bobby had said anything.

We rode the rest of the way in silence. Touchy silence.

When Bobby got out of the car, he didn't say "Break it" or even "See you." He just went into his house.

Chapter Eighteen

By Friday, we were all pretty well blocked, and pretty well scared. Gillinger went off on us for the smallest things, things we all knew he shouldn't have worried about at this point. Even Phil Hormel got the edge of his tongue a few times.

But it was Edmund he focused on, like a sniper. To hear Gillinger tell it, there was nothing he could do right. First it would be "Stop waving your arms like a gay banshee in heat," and then it was "For God's sake, stop holding yourself in like that. The audience is paying to see live actors, not dead ones."

Me he left pretty much alone, except in the scenes I had with Edmund. Then, nothing I did was right, either.

"Damn it, Hoberman, try to act like you're falling in love," he said the first time we did the balcony scene. When we re-did it, it was "Could you possibly act like you're glad to see him, at least? Jesus Christ."

Bobby got told off for being too aggressive, then for being a pansy who acted like he didn't want to fight anybody, let alone a big, tough guy like Romeo. Drew was too cute, then too formal. Once Gillinger even noticed Vivian and told her to act sexier, even though she was only walking in the party scene. She came on again swinging her hips, and he shouted at her to stop trying to call attention to herself.

By the end of the week, it felt like we were in prison camp. But, unlike prison camp, we at least had a cast party to look forward to.

This week's party was at Phil Hormel's place, an old Spanish-style home in what had been a nice neighborhood back when the house was new. Now the street wasn't so great. There were bail bondsmen and halfway houses on the corners, and some of the houses, including Phil's, had bars on the windows. The neighborhood was bad enough that some kids had been told they couldn't come. I was hoping Vivian would be among them. But no such luck. Her Mom was coming, so her daughter would be there.

My mom had been okay with it, just. "I don't like what little I know about Phil, and that part of town isn't good," she'd said. "But Edmund will go no matter what. So I guess you'd better tag along and try to protect him from any more piano-size mistakes."

Ah, yes. Protect Edmund from mistakes. If only.

Phil's house was huge. The living room was almost the size of an Olympic swimming pool, and the arched passage into the dining room made it look even bigger. There were at least five bedrooms, including the one that had been for a maid, once upon a time. There was even a basement, which was where the party was. Phil had turned it into a wine cellar, with two floor-to-ceiling racks for bottles running along the walls. Red-and-blue flashing Christmas lights were strung along the tops of the wine racks. Overhead hung a piñata shaped like a devil's head and painted red.

The ceiling was so low, and the head was so big that people kept bumping into it. Whenever they did, the devil giggled. Phil had installed some kind of electric thingie that was pressure-sensitive or something. As the place filled up, the devil made more and more sounds until it was like he was chatting along with everybody else.

There were six half-barrels filled with ice and drinks. There were little signs on sticks poking up from the ice that said either NICE or NAUGHTY. NICE meant nonalcoholic and NAUGHTY meant beer.

The room went on filling up, and pretty soon there wasn't room to move. The devil kept giggling and giggling.

At the back of the cellar, Phil and Gillinger stood side by side sipping a bottle of wine. They were the only ones drinking it, and everyone knew that they were the only ones who would be. Even in the crowded cellar, they stood a little apart from the rest of us.

Edmund was leaning against one of the wine racks with a can of NICE in one hand and an arm around Vivian. Bobby was kissing Stacy, one of the servant/citizens.

I was across the room, next to Drew, trying to keep Edmund in sight and wondering why I was bothering. The air was thick and heavy and made me slightly sick.

Edmund and Vivian threw a lip-lock on each other that looked like a permanent condition.

It made me feel like I was being stabbed in the stomach. I had to get out of there before I threw up.

"Are you okay, Miri?" Drew asked.

"Juliet's asphyxiating," I said. "Gotta get some air."

"I'll go with you," he said.

"I also have to pee."

"Okayyy—you're on your own."

I pushed and "excuse me'd" my way to the stairs and up them. Just getting out of that cellar was a big help.

I looked around for the bathroom—like a lot of old houses, Phil's only had one—and finally found it down a long hall, stuck between two of the bedrooms. On the way, I got a better look at the décor. On most of the walls hung pictures of Phil in various costumes. There he was, much younger and thinner in *Cats,* so that story was true.

There were also pictures of him in productions of *Our Town, Inherit the Wind, The Man Who Came to Dinner* and portraits of him all in black as Hamlet, and all in white as Jesus. He'd grown a beard for that one. It had hidden his underslung chin, but he still looked exactly like Phil Hormel. I doubted if anybody who'd ever played Jesus had looked less like what Jesus was supposed to look like.

But the bathroom, thank God, was empty. I sat down gratefully on the toilet seat.

Slowly, I got control of my stomach. By the time somebody knocked on the door, I was almost better.

But no matter what Mom had said about sticking near Edmund in case he needed interference run, I couldn't go back in that basement. At least not right away. I went out onto the front porch.

Maria Brandstedt was there, sitting on the steps and smoking a thin brown cigarette in a black holder. I caught a whiff of the tobacco smoke—not the thing I needed in my lungs at the moment, thanks—and twisted to go back in. But Maria heard me and turned around.

"My smoking annoys you? I'll put it out."

"Oh, you don't—" I began, but she had already crushed the cigarette against the concrete.

"Thanks," I said, and sat down beside her.

"You are not well?" she said.

"Just a little woozy all of a sudden. Guess there's not enough air down there for me."

"It's not surprising. There is hardly enough oxygen for Gillinger and Hormel to keep their egos alive, let alone enough for thirty other people to breathe." She hunched forward and wrapped her arms around her legs. "I hate parties."

"So why did you come?"

She gave me a long look. Then she said, "To keep an eye on Phil."

"Oh," I said, as if I knew what she was talking about.

"We're having an affair," she added.

"Oh," I said again.

"It's a stupid thing to do." She shrugged. "But sometimes it is absolutely necessary to be stupid, you know?"

I didn't know what to say to that.

"Stupid to care so much about some damned man. A coward and a liar, like all of them. But what else is there to do? Everything wears off after five years or so. Then it is time to love again, you know?"

I must have given something off, because Maria smiled a little and said, "Is Edmund your first?"

"Oh, we're not—" I started. Then I said, "Yes," because he was.

"So my daughter has competition. Well, you could do worse. He is a handsome rogue." She shook her head. "The two of you. Men."

Part of me wanted to straighten her out about me. But a smarter part thought, *I'm just about to find out stuff I want to know.* So I tried to look like I was The Other Woman.

Maria smiled a little. "Your mother. How does she feel about this?"

"She's okay with it so far," I said.

"Well. That is intelligent, I think. When a girl reaches your age a parent cannot really impose her will anymore."

"How does your husband feel about Vivian and Edmund?" I asked.

"Furious. But do not worry. There is nothing he can do, and he knows it." She sighed. "We make life interesting for him, my daughter and I. But without us, he would have no life at all, and he knows this."

"Do you think he knows about you and Phil?"

"Of course he knows. I am not some child to keep my love life secret from my husband," Maria said.

All of a sudden I was feeling very sorry for Mr. Brandstedt. I sat silently for a while, feeling sad for him and miserable for myself and wishing I could do something about any of it.

"Well, thanks for talking to me, Maria," I said finally. "I think I'll go back to the party."

Maria took out another cigarette.

When I got back to the basement, Edmund and Vivian were gone.

"Where's Edmund?" I asked Drew.

"Not sure," he said. "He was talking with Phil. Then he took off with Vivian."

"You just let him leave? I'm supposed to keep an eye on him. You're supposed to help me."

"He didn't ask my permission.... But if you want my opinion, they didn't go far."

"Thanks a lot," I said, and went over to Bobby.

"Bobby, do you know where Edmund and Vivian are?" I said when he and Stacy came up for air.

"I do not know, and I do not care," Bobby said.

I saw Phil with his empty glass hanging from his fingers. Gillinger was turned away, talking to Bill Meisinger.

"Hey, Phil, have you seen my cousin?" I asked.

"I gave him the key to my guesthouse," he said. "I never use it. And he and Vivian looked desperate."

"Oh. Thanks," I said, and felt my heart break.

I wanted to get out of there, to go home, to go anywhere. And I really, really didn't want to cry, which was just what I was going to do. Damn it, what were all these people doing here when I needed privacy, a lot of privacy?

I got out of the basement and made my way to the far corner of the yard and sat down with my back against a tree. I put my face on my knees and I wept.

After a while I heard quiet steps. Steps were the last thing I wanted to hear.

"Miri?"

"Leave me alone, Drew," I said.

"Take you home?" he asked.

"Yeah. I want to get out of here."

He held out his hand, but I got up on my own.

"Let's go this way," he said, and he led me to the front yard by the side of the house opposite the driveway. It was just a narrow dark little corridor with nobody there except a couple kissing. I couldn't even see who they were. Which meant they couldn't see me. Which was perfect.

Drew and I walked across the front yard with our heads down like we were talking. We turned up the street to his car. He opened the door for me and we got in.

"I'm sorry I was obtuse back there in the cellar," Drew said.

I shook my head. "Forget it."

Drew concentrated on his driving. Neither of us said anything else until he pulled into my driveway. Then we had one of those awkward moments when he came around to open the door for me and I got out without waiting for him.

"Oh," he said.

I stepped past him.

"I'm going back to the party, I guess. I'll try to keep an eye on him for you." Drew shrugged.

"He's fine," I said and then headed for the front door. "Thanks for getting me out of there."

"Miri—" he said to my back.

"Yeah?" I said without turning around.

"Miri, is there anything I can do?"

"No. Not unless you can send a certain English lout back to where he came from." I didn't mean it. But then again, part of me did. Conflicted, Dad would have said.

Drew pretended to laugh and said, "I'll work on it."

It was awkward hanging on to my doorknob. "You're a good friend, Drew. Good night."

"Miri," Drew said again.

"Yeah, Drew?" I said.

"…nothin'. Good night."

"Yeah," I said. "See you."

I went into the house and locked the door behind me. For some reason I thought about the fact that I'd never heard Drew say "nothin'" before.

Chapter Nineteen

Edmund didn't come back until almost dawn. I heard Vivian's car pull up and drive away, and he came into the house by the front door and went straight to his room. I didn't see him until that afternoon.

Mom was in the backyard weeding the flowers. I was staring at the TV without watching it.

"How was the party?" I asked as chipper as I could.

"Grand and glorious," Edmund said. He sounded really tired. "Phil Hormel is a true friend."

"Nice of Vivian to bring you back. I kind of thought she'd keep you."

"She would an she could," Edmund said. "And if I would let her. But I mind what ye said to me, faithful spirit. I'll not trust her too far."

"Well." I shrugged. "I guess it doesn't really matter very much. Sorry I was so snarky about it at first."

"Snarky! Ha, ha. Excellent word," Edmund said.

I got up.

"Mom's in the back. I need to ask her something," I said, and left him standing in the living room.

Mom was down on her knees by the tulips. There was a pile of small green dead things with their roots covered with dirt lying beside her.

"Edmund's back."

"I know," Mom said.

I watched her work. She had a metal-tipped thing like a sort of fork in her hand and she was gouging the earth around the weeds like she was a surgeon.

Out came the weed, a long-rooted monster. She tossed it onto the pile.

"Mom," I said. "Why are men such jerks?"

She brushed her hair away from her face and looked up at me.

"Honey, if I knew that, I'd write the book on it and every woman in the world would buy two copies. One for herself and one for her daughter."

She went back to digging, ferociously.

"Whew. I haven't had a chance to do this for a long time," she said. "Pulling double shifts doesn't leave a lot of time for pulling weeds."

"It's looking great."

"There's one thing I do know," Mom said. "A guy—a lot of guys—try to find out what they can get away with. What the woman will put up with. It's important for us to know what we will and won't accept."

"What about guys?" I said, thinking of Mr. Brandstedt. "Do they have to figure out what they'll accept?"

"Same thing, I guess. I've never been a guy so I can't be sure."

Then I said, "What if you love the guy?"

"All the more reason to know what you'll accept."

I got down beside my mom. "Dad went away," I said.

"Yep," she agreed. "And I'm putting up with that. And I'm still hoping he'll come back. But if he'd had another woman instead of wandering off, I'd have taken this and stuck it in his...eye."

She stabbed her weeding stick into the ground.

"Mom, were you ever in a situation where you loved somebody and he didn't love you?"

"Sure," she said.

"What did you do?"

"The question is, what are you going to do?"

What was I willing to put up with from Edmund because I loved him? Particularly when we weren't together and he was with some other girl?

"Does Edmund know how you feel?" she asked.

Did Edmund know? Let's see. Mom knew. And Drew knew. And Maria knew. And if Maria knew then Vivian did. And Bobby probably—okay, maybe the immediate world knew. But Edmund, I was sure, looked at me and saw a fairy, or a sprite, or a cuz—anything but a girl who loved him.

"No, I guess not," I said.

"You know. There's another play Shakespeare wrote around 1597. *Much Ado About Nothing.* I played Beatrice. She was in that kind of situation and she handled it pretty well."

"What did she do?"

"She never gave the guy a break," Mom said. "She made fun of him. And she had a mouth on her. You might want to try that."

"Much Ado About Nothing," I pondered aloud. "I'll take a look at it."

So I went back into the house.

Edmund was curled up on the couch snoring softly. He

looked so handsome, so sweet with his mouth open and his head thrown back so I could see his missing molars.

When I caught myself thinking that, I found *The Riverside Shakespeare* and flipped it open to page 361, then carried the book into my room.

I saw what Mom meant at once. Benedick and Beatrice are crazy about each other and they rag on each other all the time because of it. Because neither of them can admit to the other how much in love they are. Because it's better than crying.

As luck would have it, I got my first chance to try it just after I finished the play. Edmund woke up when I came back into the living room.

"Ah. Did I fall asleep?" he said.

"If that wasn't you snoring then there's a sick pig with a hell of a cold in here."

Edmund looked stunned. Then he laughed.

"And when did ye learns so much of pigs, cuz? Was it when ye were herding the Gadarene swine?" Then he laughed again and kicked his feet in the air.

"I'm sure that was very funny back in Stratford," I said.

"Have ye never heard of the Gadarene swine?" Edmund said. "They were the pigs into which Our Lord sent the legion of demons so they rushed over a cliff and were killed."

"See? I knew there was a laugh in there somewhere," I said.

"And with my good help, ye'll come to find it in a month or so."

"And without your help, I'll find it even sooner."

Edmund laughed again.

Well, if I couldn't be Juliet, Beatrice wasn't a bad default. Edmund and I slung zingers at each other all night long.

And it was better than crying.

Chapter Twenty

Monday, Drew swung by to pick up Edmund and me, and there was no Bobby with him.

"Where's Tybalt?" I asked as I got into the front seat.

"Coming on his own," Drew said. "That's what he told me."

Drew without Bobby. That was new.

"Tybalt without Mercutio," Edmund mused. "The play is out of balance."

"Nay, 'tis cool. Bobby's mad, but I think he's kind of enjoying acting it. He'll probably go on to something else before too long."

But if Bobby was acting, he turned out to be giving it everything he had. He strolled in to rehearsal with one of the girls just before we started. He sauntered past Drew like he didn't see him. The girl brought him the roll of blue masking tape and he slowly wound some around his right arm. When rehearsal began, he made his first entrance with his head and shoulders forward, ready for a fight.

He gave his first line. Then, he shoved the kid playing one of the Capulet servants and the poor little guy fell down.

"Hey, dude," the servant said from the floor.

"Deal with it," Bobby said, and went into his sword-fight stance.

The kid got up. Then one of the Montague servants pushed him down again.

The other Capulet servant pushed back.

"Dude, what are you doing?" the first Capulet said.

Bobby didn't answer. He just lunged, like he had a sword, and snaked his leg around and tripped the guy he'd pushed.

Then all five boys, the Capulet and Montague servants and Bobby were shoving each other.

It didn't feel like improv. It felt like a fight.

"Cut!" Gillinger roared. "What is this supposed to be?"

"Trying to put some energy into the scene," Bobby said. "It's slow. Maybe you've noticed."

"Of course it's slow," Gillinger said. "You don't know it yet. Now apologize."

"Sorry," Bobby said, to nobody in particular.

We went on. Eventually, we got to the party scene where Romeo and Juliet first see each other. Everybody's supposed to be masked.

Bobby came in, same way as before, walked over to Edmund and pretended to pull off Edmund's mask.

"Capulet bastard," he said. Then he slapped Edmund. Hard.

For a moment Edmund just stood there. Then he threw a punch that would have dropped Bobby had it connected, but Bobby dodged it and danced around the stage.

"What the hell?" Gillinger said. "What the hell are you doing?"

"Subtext," Bobby said. "Like you taught us in class."

"Stick to the script!" Gillinger snapped.

Edmund dropped his hand to his side, but it was still clenched. "What are you playing at, Bobby?"

"What's the matter, dude? Don't they do subtext in England?"

Edmund was furious. He touched his cheek and glared at Bobby. Bobby was still dancing on the balls of his feet, getting madder and madder.

"Subtext. It's what's really going on in a scene," Bobby said. "Not just a bunch of words and blocking. You know—acting."

"Damn it, Ruspoli, I am directing this play," Gillinger said.

"I wondered who was. When do you plan to start?"

"Ruspoli, outside. Now," Gillinger spat.

The two of them left the theater. The rest of us stood around wondering what was going on.

"Just like *Miss Saigon,*" Phil Hormel said. It was all anybody said out loud.

After about twenty years, Bobby and Gillinger came back in. They weren't walking together. Gillinger strode in and threw himself down on his throne. Bobby followed him, still stalking like he wanted to fight.

"Ruspoli has something he wants to say," Gillinger announced.

"Sorry, everybody," Bobby said, center stage. "I overdid it. I know that. But this show, it's important to me, you know? And now there's this Ashland thing. I mean, we've got make it good, you know? I'm just trying to make it good. Sorry if that wasn't clear."

As apologies went, it was more of a brush-off. And I don't think anyone believed a word of it.

But Gillinger said, "Understood, Ruspoli. Now let's get back to work."

Ever wonder what Verona was like with all those Capulets and Montagues running around killing each other? A little tense, maybe. Like you didn't know what was going to happen next, or who was going to be the target. That was what the rest of that night was like.

And Edmund was still smoldering from the smack Bobby had given him. He wanted to get back at him. He had more sense than to hit him, but he thought of another way.

As soon as Gillinger called break, Edmund grabbed Vivian, threw his arms around her and kissed her hard, right in front of Bobby. Actually, it was in front of everybody, including me. But Bobby was his audience.

When Edmund let her go, she staggered backward and eeped,

"Oh, speak again, bright angel."

And kissed him back.

And probably that was why the balcony scene was absolutely no good at all that night. No, to be fair, Edmund wasn't bad. I was what was absolutely no good. I kept blowing my lines, stumbling over words. And the farther we went, the worse I got. It was like I'd never seen the scene before.

And Gillinger let me know it. "Hoberman, we are too far along at this point for you to be this incompetent," he said, interrupting me just as Edmund was about to climb up and join me. "Take it from the top."

And I did, and I was better but still no good. We made it to the end of the scene and Gillinger snarled that it was time to quit, even though we had nearly an hour left.

"For God's sake, go home and use the extra time to learn your lines," he said.

We all started to leave. I saw Bobby and Drew talking in the corner. Bobby shook his head at something Drew said, and waved his hand at me and Edmund. Then he went off with Girl of the Week.

"May I give you a ride home?" Drew asked me and Edmund.

His formality surprised me. Usually Drew just came over and said, "Need a ride?" or something like that.

But Vivian was already standing in Edmund's shadow.

"Vivian will bring me home," Edmund said. "We'll not be late."

"But don't wait up," Vivian said, smiling.

I was sure they were heading for Phil's guesthouse.

"Say hello to the roaches for me," I said in my best Beatrice.

"We will. For we know they are particular friends of yours," Edmund said, smiling.

They went off with their arms around each other.

Maria saw me looking after them and smiled a smile that was supposed to say something world-weary in German, I guess.

When we reached his car, Drew opened the door for me.

"You don't have to do that."

"Sorry," Drew said.

"Don't be sorry, just don't do it," I snapped. Then I said, "Sorry."

I could tell I'd hurt Drew's feelings, so I said, "It was nice of you. If I were out on a date and a guy didn't do it, he'd get marked down. Big black 'X' in the datebook. But we're just—going home, you know?"

"Yeah," Drew said.

"So what's Bobby doing?" I asked. "Is he trying to get

Gillinger to throw him out? Is he so ticked off that he can't play Romeo that he wants to quit?"

"No. Bobby's a lot smarter than that. And he's a lot angrier than I realized. I think what he's trying to do is to build on what Gillinger's doing already. Mess with everybody's head, make everyone nervous and afraid, and ruin the show. Do whatever he can to guarantee that we're bad. The Revenge of Tybalt, in real life."

"No way," I said. "Bobby's a total theater boy. He'd never mess up a show like that."

"Dudes can do unexpected things sometimes. And it's the theory that makes the most sense," Drew said. "I've never seen him this mad."

"Oh, Drew, I'm sorry. Why's he mad at you…if it's any of my business?"

"Why do you think?" Drew said. "He thinks I'm freezing him out now that Edmund's around. He thinks there's some big secret that he's not part of, and of course he's right."

In the come-and-go glare of the streetlights we drove under, I could see Drew's face was pained.

My own hurt made me feel closer to him. On an impulse I reached out and put my hand on his shoulder.

"It's really great what you're doing," I said. "And I really appreciate it. I know Edmund does, too. It's huge, actually."

"Always glad to help," Drew said, trying to make it sound offhand.

We were pulling into our driveway now. Drew turned off his engine, but I didn't get out.

"What do you think's going to happen?" I asked.

"I don't know. There are too many possibilities. Everything's in play all of a sudden."

And right that moment, for that moment, Drew was my

best friend. Things happen like that in theater. And usually they happen when things are going badly.

"Have you got time to talk?" I said.

"Sure," he said.

And then I spilled my guts about Edmund, and Edmund-and-Vivian and how much I wanted to play Juliet to give the performance to my mom. Sitting in the dark in his silly little car, I told Drew Jenkins as much about my heart as if he'd been a girl and we'd been total BFF since kindergarten. And it felt totally right and okay to do it because it was Drew.

When I was finished, I said, "I haven't talked that much in a long time. Thanks."

"Sure. You're welcome. Glad to do it."

"Listen," I said. "Don't take this the wrong way—that's stupid, I know you won't—but you are really great, man. Globally great. If I can ever help you the way you just helped me tonight, or anything else I can do, just ask. Okay?"

Drew didn't say anything for a long moment. Then he said, "Well there is one thing. Don't take it the wrong way."

"What?" I said.

"Let me open your door for you."

"Okay," I said. "Just because it's you."

And Drew got out of his car and walked around and opened my door. I slid out, gave his arm a squeeze, and said, "Good night, oh awesome one."

"Good night, Juliet," Drew said.

Chapter Twenty-One

Bobby didn't pull any more stunts like the Monday Night Slap Fest, but he gave off the energy that said that he might, and that was even better for keeping the rest of us on edge than the real thing would have been. Edmund never turned his back on him. Gillinger snarled at everybody more than usual, especially Edmund. Maybe he was trying to keep the lid on things. If so, it wasn't working. In fact we were dividing into Edmundites, Gillingerites and a few Bobbyites. It was getting ugly.

When rehearsals were over, Bobby took off with a girl named Maggie Brown and Edmund took off with Vivian. He came home late, tiptoed into bed and slept until noon. I hardly saw him except at rehearsals the rest of the week. When I did, I made sure to keep my Beatrice up.

"Ah, my lord. I see that thou art red of eye and feeble of body. Could it be that thou art something too old for the life thou art leading?" I said when I came home Friday and saw him lying on the couch.

"Withered crone, thou speaks't of matters beyond thy

ken." He laughed. "Come and see the reason why thou finds't me reposing in rest richly earned."

And he levered himself up and took me to the back of the house.

"Thy good mother and I speak of many things of which you know naught," he said. "And one of these is her gardens. Exit, and behold."

I went out the back door and was blown away by what I saw. Everything Mom hadn't had a chance to do with her flowers was done, and from what I could tell, it was done better than she knew how. The small trees were trimmed. The lawn was mowed. And more than all of these, there was an air of precision about the yard that had never been there before.

"'Tis thus I have been spending my time, fair dudess," he said to me. "For a Warwickshireman is the finest gardener since Adam, and I mean to earn my keep. D'ye think your mother will be pleased?"

"I think she'll plotz," I said.

"Plotz?" Edmund said.

"Faint," I said. "Dang, man, you work fast!"

It was beautiful, but I almost wished he hadn't done it. It made my love for him flow over me, and I didn't want that. So instead I said, "'Tis wondrous to find there's something you're good at besides sleeping and eating."

And then Mom came home a little later and when she saw the yard she hugged Edmund and kissed him on the cheek, and damn it, I even felt jealous of her for a second.

Phil called another party at his place on Friday night. Most of the older actors didn't go. Maybe they had some other place to hang, maybe they were just sick of Gillinger, Bobby and the tension. Anyway, they weren't in his big old house in the bad part of town that night. Apart from Phil, Maria and Gillinger himself, everyone there was a kid. I noticed that we all pretty much grouped into Capulets in the backyard and Montagues in the front. Nobody was down in the basement because that would have meant mingling.

I, however, was down there, looking for Drew. I thought that maybe we could have another long, intimate talk that would make the time pass until he drove me home.

But the basement was empty except for the grinning piñata devil. For no reason, I lay down on the floor and looked up at it.

Edmund and Vivian came down the steps.

"Alas, fair cuz, are ye dead?" Edmund said when he saw me. "If so, the devil must fear for his throne."

"The only devil down here is the one up there," I said. "I'm just lying here wondering why he looks so much like you."

Edmund laughed. He always appreciated my zingers.

I started to get up. Those two were going to start playing tonsil hockey and Beatrice wasn't interested in watching that.

As I got to my feet, I heard angry voices. Excited voices. And the word, "Fight, fight."

Suddenly, everyone was running, sauntering, trotting, from the backyard to the front. Capulets joined a ring of Montagues on the front lawn where Bobby Ruspoli was circling, and swinging and shouting at someone. At Drew.

And Drew was fighting back, sort of. He was blocking Bobby's punches, ducking and backpedaling, but not really hitting.

The people in the ring were shouting, "Go, Tybalt," "Go, Bobby," "Death to Mercutio," "I don't believe it," or were just flat-out laughing.

Bobby swung his right fist in a wild arc that connected with Drew's, which had clearly been connected with a few times already. This time, Drew's face was involved. Blood spurted out.

I broke through the circle and pushed myself between them. Bobby slugged my boob by accident.

"Get outta my way," he shouted, while Drew tried to push me from behind.

"You two jerks cut it out!" I yelled. "Either cut it out or hit me again, 'cause I ain't leavin'. And, Edmund, stay out of it."

Because, of course, he was right there, grinning like an angry wolf at Bobby.

"He hit ye," Edmund shouted.

"It's all your God damn fault," Bobby said, and started toward Edmund.

I spun around with my arms out, trying to keep the three of them apart.

"By God, it shall be my fault," Edmund roared and tried to punch Bobby over my shoulder which resulted in me getting a lightning bolt to my jaw, snapping my head back and knocking me to the ground.

"Shit!" said Bobby

"Damn!" said Edmund.

"Miri!" Drew said.

Well, I stopped the fight.

They all got down beside me and Edmund lifted me gently by my shoulders.

"Oh, God. Oh, God," Edmund was saying. "God damn me for a whoreson. Oh, Miri."

"We gotta talk," I said as well as I could. "In private. Me, you. And these two jerks. Now."

"Right," Drew said. "As soon as I get a nose rag."

"What about me?" Vivian said.

"Wait for me," Edmund said.

"Say, what?" Vivian snarled.

"I say, wait," Edmund repeated.

"Like hell," Vivian said.

Edmund looked surprised. "These are friends," he said. "And there is much amiss here. Let me do what I can and I will come back as soon as I may."

"You came with me to this party. You're not going off with her," Vivian said.

"I say I am," Edmund told her.

"Damn it, you're always keeping secrets from me," Vivian said. "And I resent it. If you go off with those twits, you're not coming back to me."

Edmund looked thoughtful. Then he bowed. "Be damned to ye then, Vivian. And good night."

Someone had brought Drew a washcloth. He cleaned off his face, including his swollen nose.

We left Vivian standing on the sidewalk while we went down the street to where Drew's car was parked. Edmund steadied me, and Bobby walked on my other side saying, "I'm sorry, Miri," and, "you should have stayed out of it" while I tried to walk straight. Damn, Edmund had a fist on him.

Drew opened the door for me and I slid into the front seat. He got in on the other side and put his head back. Bobby and Edmund stood on the sidewalk.

"Now. What. The. *Hell?*" I said.

"It's my fault," Drew said through his washcloth. "But I'm not quite sure why."

"The hell you're not," Bobby said.

"You asked me where Vivian was, and I said, 'Attached to Edmund's hip same as always.' And you started slugging me," Drew said.

"It's not just about Vivian," Bobby said. "Look, I know

there's some big-ass secret about Edmund. I don't care. I don't care if he's an illegal alien from England or an illegal alien from Mars. I don't give a damn. What I do give a damn about is you and Miri and him treating me like I can't be trusted. Like I'd blab to everybody. That is bullshit, man. Because if there is one thing you know about me, Jenkins, it is that I can keep a secret."

Drew took the washcloth away from his face. "I'm sorry," he said. "You're right."

He looked at his friend like a dog that's bitten you and is trying to apologize.

"It's my fault, Bobby," I said. "I made Drew promise."

"I shouldn't have," Drew said.

"'Tis my fault," Edmund said.

"Look, like I said. I don't care what the big secret is," Bobby said. "If you'd just said, 'There's something going on that I can't tell you about 'cause I promised Miri I wouldn't,' that would have been cool. But you didn't even do that."

"You're right," Drew said. "I'm a rat."

"At least," Bobby said.

"Okay. I'm a rat bastard," Drew said.

"Yeah," Bobby said, and his shoulders dropped. "But you're a pretty cool rat bastard underneath."

"Thanks," Drew said.

"Bobby, I would tell ye the truth now if ye would care to hear it," Edmund said.

Bobby shrugged. "Like I said. Not important."

"Not to ye, maybe," Edmund said. "But I would have ye for a friend, a true friend, if ye will have me for yours. And to such a friend I must open myself. What say ye?"

"Sure. Whatever."

"But first I must tell ye that Vivian knows nothing of it,"

Edmund said. "Nor can she. Fond as I am of her, I know she is loose-tongued. But ye, as ye say, are a man for secrets."

Bobby stood there, a man for secrets, waiting for Edmund to go on.

So Edmund did.

And when he was done, all Bobby could say was, "Man. That is so cool." And half hugged him. Then he said, "You really Shakespeare's brother?"

"Aye. The ass of the world and I came out of the same mother," Edmund said.

I started to laugh, but my jaw hurt too much. "Ow. You know, I don't feel much like going back to that party right now."

"Me, either," Drew said.

"Plus, you're all covered with blood," Bobby said.

"Let's take you back to the house and get you cleaned up," I said. "And then maybe we could all go somewhere quiet together."

When we got back to Phil's house, everyone came out on the lawn to see us. Nobody knew how to react. Then I kissed Bobby on the cheek, and he hugged Drew and Edmund hugged Bobby, and the cast cheered and clapped.

All but Vivian.

"She took off in a snit," Tanya Blair said. "She left me with a message for Edmund. Politely rephrased it's something like, 'if you don't call and apologize tomorrow, forget about—uh—dating me ever again.'"

"Harsh," Bobby said, looking slightly happy.

"Ah, well," Edmund said.

We went into the house. Bobby gave Drew his jacket to cover the bloody shirt. I took a couple of aspirins for my throbbing jaw. Then, with Bobby riding shotgun and Edmund and me in the back, we took off for an hour drive around quiet streets.

It was one of those truly great drives. By the time it was over, the only things that weren't healed were Drew's nose and my jaw. But our relationships had undergone major surgery, and the patients were doing well.

Chapter Twenty-Two

It is a great thing to have a mother who is a nurse. Because when she saw my jaw she knew just what to do about it. She put some stuff on it to draw out the swelling, taped me up and gave me a painkiller that was stronger than aspirin. I slept hard, and when I woke up, it was late Saturday afternoon.

I didn't tell Mom exactly how I had gotten the jaw. That would have been Too Much Information. I just said there'd been a fight, I'd tried to stop it, and someone had slugged me by accident.

Mom let it go at that. But she did tell me I wasn't going to any more parties at Phil's.

Edmund was working outside, all sweaty and wonderful. He had seen some agapanthus flowers in a neighbor's yard and told Mom that she must have some, too. So she'd bought the plants and he was making a new bed for them in the middle of the front yard.

It was amazing to see Edmund use tools. It was like they became part of him. And he sang while he worked. And

Mom, who worked much more slowly, was happy digging in the flowers along the front of the house, knowing wonderful things were getting done behind her back.

It was a warm, misty afternoon, and I thought something to drink would complete the picture. So I made a pitcher of iced tea and one of lemonade with lemons from our own tree, and brought them out.

"These drinks ye make are fine and strange," Edmund said after he'd drained his third glass of my, admittedly amazing, tea. "I like them well, better than colas."

"I gotta tell you, Edmund," my mom said. "If Doctor Dee ever figures out how to get you back to England and Good Queen Bess, he's going to have to deal with me. This place never looked so spiffy."

"It pleasures me to do it," Edmund said. "To find that there is yet something I can do well, is a comfort. I was always the best gardener among the Shakespeares, so our mother said."

His face grew very serious. I was sure he was thinking about England.

"But, no, I would not go home if I could," he said. "No longer. I have hopes here that I may rise higher as an actor than ever I could there. Greatly do I miss those I left behind. But—anyway, 'tis impossible."

Well. Edmund and Vivian were on the outs *and* he wanted to stay here. This was turning out to be a pretty good day.

"Welcome home, cuz," I said, and hugged him.

After a couple more hours of picturesque gardening scenes, Bannerman called, asking if Mom could come in and work in surgery. They were short a nurse and it had to be done ASAP. Of course, she said yes. She hurried off to the hospital and Edmund and I were left alone.

The sun was going behind the rooftops now. Evening was coming on. I felt my blissful little mood of late afternoon turning into the sadness I usually felt when day turned into night. Dad said this was a perfectly normal feeling, that our species was so well adapted to daylight that the loss of it made us unhappy. Most mammals see better in twilight. We don't.

All very interesting, but not helpful. I wished I had a theater to go to and some work to do there. I got up.

"I'm going to do something about dinner," I said. "You hungry?"

"I could eat a bear!"

"I'll see if we have some in the freezer."

I made chicken tacos and a salad. Edmund wolfed them down.

"There is somewhat I would tell thee, cuz," he said, laying down his fork.

"If 'tis that my cooking is the best ye've ever tasted, I know that already," I said.

He smiled. "'Tis only that I hate myself for what I did to ye last night," he said.

"Edmund, it was an accident," I said.

"Of course it was," he said. "And yet, ye're hurt, and I did it."

Hurt. Oh, Edmund, if you only knew.

"No, really. It's not that bad. I'm a fast healer. Look. Practically gone already."

I pulled the tape off my face.

He reached out and touched me very gently.

"I hit ye very hard.... Yet now there is scarce a mark to be seen."

"Wonders of modern medicine," I said. "Also, my neck took a lot of the force. I'll probably have blinding headaches for the rest of my life, but my bruise is small."

"Oh, cuz," Edmund said.

"I'm joking," I said. "I'll be fine. I am fine."

"I feel I must do something to make my apology, all the same. Is there nothing ye would command me to do, fair cuz, like some great lady of old romance to her knight?"

I think he was in more pain than I was. It made me hurt for him. But how could Beatrice comfort Benedick without dropping her guard?

Then it came to me.

"Actually, there is one thing you could do." I smiled evilly. "One thing, and one thing only, O, wannabe knight." I pointed to the kitchen sink. "The dishes."

Edmund looked shocked.

"I could never do so womanly a thing!" he said. "Command me something else."

"Nope," I said. "I mean, nay, varlet. Have at them."

Edmund looked at his big, strong hands. He shook his head. Then his face took the set of a man who was going to jump off a cliff to prove he could do it.

"I will do this," he said. "But promise me, cuz, ye will not torment me nor mention it to anyone. I cannot help finding it unmanly."

"I promise."

"Will ye help me?"

"I'll *advise* you."

"What must I do?" he asked.

"First, pick up the things on the table and transfer them to the kitchen without dropping them."

Edmund took every dish into the kitchen one at a time.

"Well done, sir knight," I said when he was finished. "Now, scrape the plates into the trash."

He did.

"Now, sirrah, fill the sink with soap and water."

He held the dish-detergent bottle in both hands and shook it up and down.

"Squeeze, good knight, squeeze," I told him.

He did, and way too much detergent fell into the sink.

"Is't enough, d'ye think?" Edmund said, and turned on the taps.

When the sink was hidden by a mountain island of suds, Edmund held up a plate.

"Nay, sir. Begin with the glasses," I said. "Cleanest to dirtiest doth make the water keep its cleansing properties the longest."

Edmund picked up a glass, studied it and daintily put it into the water.

"How long must I leave it there?" he asked.

"Oh, 'twill not clean itself. Scrub, sir, scrub. The small blue squarish thing is your tool."

Slowly, as carefully as if he were washing a baby, Edmund ran the sponge over the glass.

"There. That's done," he said, and rinsed it.

"Nobly done, sir," I told him.

I decided to do the fair thing and dry it.

One by one, Edmund washed the dishes. While he worked he sang a sad song about a girl who'd drowned herself in the Avon River when her boyfriend dumped her.

"And her dress did float
And her hands did float,
And her hair did float about her."

That was the chorus.

It was a really awful song. And he handed me things to dry in time with it.

Finally, I joined in on the chorus. I took the salad bowl and sang,

"And her dress did float
And her hands did float
And her hair did float about her."

I waved the dish towel slowly back and forth like it was the hem of the drowned girl's dress.

"Ah, cuz. Ye sing most affectingly," Edmund said. "Stop, I beg you, before I am unmanned completely by yer howls."

Then I realized he'd been playing with me.

"Thou rogue," I said, laughing. "Thou hast been having me on. Thou art no more afraid of these dishes than thou art of thine own pillow."

"D'ye think I do not watch all ye do?" Edmund grinned. "Ye teach me much, cuz, and never know it."

"Aw, I'll bet you say that to all the fairies," I said. Then I giggled like an idiot and dropped my dish towel.

Edmund picked it up and handed it back to me.

"I thank thee, fair knight," I said. "In fact, I dub thee Sir Edmund of Warwickshire, Knight of the Blue Sponge."

There was a bread knife in the dish rack. I took it and touched him on each shoulder.

He looked at me the way Romeo must have looked at Juliet when he saw her for the first time. Then he put his lips on mine, and I took his beautiful face between my hands and ran my fingers through his long, chestnut hair.

I was falling and flying, and I knew that I could hold him forever if he wanted me to.

But then he pushed himself away, and he was blushing.

"Oh, Miri, I am sorry," he said. "Do not think on this.

I was—I was—" and he ran into his room and slammed the door.

What did I do now?

My feet decided for the rest of me. I followed him.

"Edmund, it's—it's okay," I said through the door. "Come on out. We need to talk about it."

"Nay," he said.

"Yes," I said.

"Talk through the door if ye must," he said.

"I'm coming in," I said.

"Nay!"

But I opened the door.

Edmund was sitting hunched up on the bed.

"Begone," he said. "Lest worse befall."

I sat down beside him.

"Get off me bed," he shouted.

"Edmund," I said. "It's all right."

"Nay, 'tis never all right," he said. "I have broken your trust and near violated your good mother's faith in me."

I gulped. "Edmund. It's okay if you feel that way about me. I feel that way, too."

"Ye do?" He looked as surprised as if I'd sprouted wings.

"Yes."

"But do not ye see how much above me ye are?" Edmund said. "Ye are an enchantress, a spirit. Almost a goddess, ye seem. When I first saw ye, I thought ye must be Helen of Troy."

"That? I thought that was because of the spell—oh, never mind. Edmund, I'm not any of those things. I'm just Miri of Guadalupe. But if you need me to be an enchantress or a goddess or anything else, I'll give it my best shot."

We kissed again, and it was better than before.

"Ah, Miri, I must not," Edmund said. "We must not. 'Tis

betrayal." He took me in his arms again and I kissed him and we fell back together and—

And the front door opened and Mom came home.

Edmund pushed me away like he'd had an electric shock. Then he pulled me back to him. Then he pushed me away again, while I tried to hold on.

"Milady!" he shouted at my mom and raced out of his room. More than a little panicked, I smoothed my hair looking in the little mirror over Edmund's bureau. I smiled. I couldn't believe how happy I looked.

Chapter Twenty-Three

I was expecting to see Mom's usual back-from-an-operation face, which was a tired but satisfied look. Instead, she looked sad and worried.

"Mom, what is it?" I said.

"Bad news, I'm afraid, Miri. Bad for you, I mean."

How could she know how could she know how could she know? was all that was going through my mind.

"That operation I was called out on? Guess who it was. Gillinger. Major heart attack. He'll live, but he won't be directing anytime soon. In fact, his directing days may be over."

I have to tell you the first thing I thought was not, *How awful for poor Mr. Gillinger,* but *Who are they going to get to replace him?* Actors do tend to be self-involved.

Anyway, Mom gave Edmund and me the details over cups of tea.

Gillinger had had his attack the night before, and hadn't been able to get to a phone. He'd just lain on the floor of his bedroom conscious but unable to move until Phil Hormel happened to stop by and found him there. If he'd been alone much longer, he would probably have died.

But all the time that passed from attack to when he was discovered was what made his case so serious.

"Poor fellow," Edmund said. "Never to do theater again. That would be worse than death, I think."

My cell phone buzzed. I took it into my room to answer it.

"They're canceling the play." Tanya Blair's voice was shaky. "They just sent me an email."

"Who's 'they'?" I asked in a squeaky voice.

"The school. The arts council. The people who funded us! They're going to shut us down."

"Shut us down? Why?"

"They say they'll explain it tomorrow night at the theater," Tanya said. "They have a meeting planned for seven o'clock tomorrow night."

"Oh, damn," I said. "Oh, damn it to hell."

"Yeah—so be there. We've got to make them change their minds."

"Yeah. Of course. Right."

I hung up. They couldn't cancel the show. Not when I needed it so badly. They couldn't take my part—my gift, my shot at Ashland, my chance to be Edmund's Juliet—away from me.

I stood in the middle of my room and let out a long, wordless wail.

Edmund was there in a second. "What is't?" he said when he saw my face.

I folded myself into his arms. "They're canceling us," I whispered. "There won't be any show."

Mom came into my room and saw us together.

"What is going on?" she said.

When I told her, she came over and joined our hug.

"Oh, honey, I'm so sorry," she said. "But that's the way it is sometimes. The arts in this country are run by a bunch of goons who don't like the arts. And now they have an excuse. Damn them. Damn them all."

"Nay," Edmund said. "That will not be the way of it."

He stepped back, held my shoulders in his beautiful strong hands, and said, "The play will open. I swear it to ye."

"What? What are you going to do?" I said. I was afraid he was going to get a sword and take it to the meeting tomorrow and run everybody on the arts council through.

"'Tis still forming in my brain. But this much I will tell ye. The man who thinks to get between me and Romeo had better never been born. I'll pray the night. Tomorrow, fight." He backed up and bowed to me. "Fear not, my Juliet."

And he went down the hall to his room. I heard the door shut.

Mom brushed away a tear and said, "Damn, that boy knows how to make an exit."

It was too much. I melted down. I cried. I cried for the play and I cried because I was in love. I cried because I couldn't talk about it. I cried because I was crying and crying was all there was.

"There, baby, there," Mom said, holding me. "This, too, shall pass."

But that's what I was afraid of. I didn't want it to pass. I wanted what I wanted and I wanted it right then. I wanted to be in Edmund's arms, and I wanted to be with him on stage under hot bright lights dazzling a theater full of people. I wanted to be Juliet, damn it. Why did that have to be so hard?

Chapter Twenty-Four

The theater felt like a tomb. Even with all of us there, the dim lights and the still air made the place seem like someone had died. Everyone was subdued, quiet, extra-nice. Worried. Probably the way the Capulets and Montagues were after they discovered the corpses of Romeo and Juliet.

Exactly at seven, two guys in suits climbed up onto the stage. One was Mr. Lawrence, the high-school principal. The other was someone I didn't know. A tall man with a bad haircut.

"Thank you all for coming out this evening," Mr. Lawrence said. "Most of you younger people know I'm Dave Lawrence, the principal here at Steinbeck. This is Ted Zecher who represents the city arts programs. As you know, Mr. Gillinger, your director, won't be able to continue directing the show. Since we got that message, Mr. Zecher has been trying to find a competent person to replace him. Mr. Zecher."

"Thanks, Mr. Lawrence," the bad haircut said. "As you know, your director Mr. Gillinger has suffered a severe heart attack. Unfortunately, that means he won't be able to continue directing this show. And since you can't have a play without a director, I'm afraid we're going to have to shut down the production."

A sort of moan ran through the cast, even though we'd known what we were going to hear. Some of us said, "No," out loud, and Bobby Ruspoli stood up.

"This is totally bullshit, man," he said. "Don't tell me you can't find somebody to take over."

"I understand that you're upset, Bobby," Mr. Lawrence put in. "You've all worked very hard."

"The point is, we can't find anyone qualified on such short notice," Mr. Zecher said.

"Let me try," Bill London said. "I know some directors. A couple up in San Francisco, a couple over in Oakland. They've got years of chops. Heck, I know people doing Equity waiver stuff in L.A. we could get. People who've directed on Broadway. Better than Gillinger."

We rippled agreement.

"Thank you very much," Zecher said. "But as I'm sure you know time is of the essence. We need somebody now, not next week. And the stipend for directing the show wouldn't be enough to get somebody from out of the area—"

"Can I at least *try?*" Bill said.

"The school and the city have taken the decision together to cancel the show," Mr. Lawrence said. "I know how disappointed many of you are. But there are probably several other shows that will be performed in the area this summer. I wish you luck in getting a part in one of them. Now, unless there are any further questions, I think it's time to bring this meeting to a close."

"Like hell it is!" Bobby Ruspoli shouted, and we all applauded.

"Isn't it simply the truth that you don't want to do the show and never did?" Phil Hormel said.

We applauded his question. Phil was right, I was sure of it. Gillinger had made Lawrence and Zecher mad when he sneered at them for not letting him do *Doctor Faustus*. This was just revenge. But it was revenge on us, not him—and we were innocent.

"Get us a director," Bobby shouted.

"This meeting is over," Mr. Lawrence said. "Thank you all for coming, and for being willing to work so hard. Please leave the building."

Edmund jumped out of his seat and leapt onto the stage. He threw out his arms and roared, "All of ye—you—give me your phone numbers. Take no new parts. I'll be in touch to tell you where we are to do this play!"

A few people cheered. A couple laughed. Most just stared at him.

Then the stage lights went out. "To the lobby," Edmund shouted, like he was leading an army. "We'll not let these counter-casting rogues stop us."

Out in the lobby the evening light was coming in through the plate-glass doors, and a lot of people came over and gave Edmund our numbers and email addresses. Not everyone, but way more than half the cast. We purposely did it slowly while Zecher and Lawrence bleated that the meeting was over and it was time to close the theater. Then, when Edmund was holding a sheaf of little pieces of paper with all the actors' info, we four walked out together, Edmund, Bobby, Drew and I.

"What's up?" Bobby said. "What are we going to do?"

"What else?" Edmund said. "We are going to do the play, dude. Just as I said."

"Where, exactly?" I wanted to know.

"Where best we may. And I know the place if we can get it. Drew, friend, will you drive us?"

"Sure," Drew said. "Where are we going?"

"Malpaso Row," Edmund said.

"Shotgun," Bobby said.

We parked in the lot at the edge of the Row and followed Edmund through the fake Italian streets.

"This whole place is but a set," Edmund said. "A sort of toy Verona where folk shop and live. And since it is a toy city, it has a toy square. Behold."

Drew, Bobby and I looked where Edmund was pointing. It was the place where the four arms of stores came together and the traffic flowed around a big hexagonal plaza with a fountain. Since it was Sunday, a lot of people were out strolling with their dogs and their babies, or sitting on the green metal benches.

"In fair Verona where we lay our scene," Edmund began, "We can set up seats on three sides of one end of the square that is not a square, build a simple, sturdy stage with discovery and balcony, and do the rest of our acting on these bricks. It could be done."

"Where would you get the money?" Bobby asked.

"I will ask the cast for it," Edmund said.

"Just like that, we're going to give you the money to do this show?" I said.

"'Tis what we did in London. A few actors with the money put up costs and then appear on the stage. If the play goes well, they prosper. The only difference is, we have no hired players here."

"I've got a thousand bucks saved up," Drew said. "You can have it."

"Wow, dude," Bobby said. Then he said. "My bike's titanium. Four thousand new. Probably get three for it."

Drew kicked into full-thinking mode. "Let's ask some of the others. If we can get a few thousand more together, we may have some cred with the management here when we go to them with the idea."

"Aye, cred. That's the thing," Edmund said. "Whatever it is, we must have it."

I couldn't believe it, but Edmund was turning into a producer before my wondering eyes. And the other thing I couldn't believe absolutely was that I believed in his ability to pull this off.

"And one more thing we must have. Kneel down with me, friends, or not, as ye are minded to do."

Edmund knelt to pray. Bobby got down on all fours at first. He thought Edmund was going to do some kind of actor's exercise. Drew shrugged and got down beside Bobby, but he understood what Edmund was doing. He folded his hands. I joined Edmund. I didn't believe any of it, but he did, and that was enough for me.

Edmund clenched his hands together. "Heavenly Father, we do implore Your blessing on our endeavors. If all the world's a stage as 'tis said, let this stage rise like a new creation, and if it be Your will, may it happen soon, for we've got only four weeks. Bless all who undertake this labor, and may our work be offered to Your greater glory. Amen."

Looking around out of the corner of my eye, I could see some people staring at us, and a little kid pointing and asking what we were doing. I kind of was wondering the same thing myself.

Edmund opened his eyes. "I dare to hope He has said yes," he declared to us. Then he got up and threw his arms around me and Drew. Drew reached out an arm and dragged Bobby in.

"Here's how it shall be," my Romeo said. "We raise the

money—we've already begun that. Then we find what we need to build the theater. Then we take the whole to whoever gives us permission to do it. This we must do in three days. Then, we build the stage, rehearse our play and do it for the multitudes who will come."

"Damn," Bobby said. "This kicks ass."

"Aye," Edmund said. "It doth."

Chapter Twenty-Five

That night, Edmund called everyone who'd given him a phone number. Amazingly, more people agreed to put up at least some money for the show. There's something about an English accent that makes anything sound reasonable to an American, I think. Anyway, by the end of the evening, he had over ten thousand dollars in pledges.

When I got to school the next morning, it was the first day of finals week. The year was ending and I'd hardly noticed. Amazingly, I sailed through my first one, biology, and even finished early. I hadn't known I liked the subject so well.

When I went out into the hall, I saw Tanya Blair. She waved and came hurrying toward me.

"This is fantastic," she said. "Is it okay if I tell my Uncle Lou?"

"Sure. You can sell him a ticket."

"No, that's not it," Tanya said. "My uncle Lou has a company. It's him and this other guy. Standing Ovation. They build sets. They've got contracts with the theaters all over this area. They could bid on the job."

To tell you the truth, I had sort of been wondering how a bunch of kids were going to build an Elizabethan theater. This sounded encouraging.

"Have him talk to Edmund," I said. "Fast."

That afternoon, when my English final was over, Edmund called me and said to meet him at the Row. When I got there, standing in the square were a couple of guys who were definitely theater types. One was short and good-looking with an elaborate beard. The other was almost a giant, dressed in a leather kilt with tools hanging off of it.

The one with the beard turned out to be Tanya's Uncle Lou.

"Well met, gentlemen," Edmund said, shaking their hands. "I'm Edmund Shakeshaft, and this is Miranda Hoberman. She plays Juliet."

"Hi, Miri," Lou said. "Glad to meet you. Tanya's said some good words about you."

"Thanks," I said. "It's great you guys want the contracts. But did Edmund tell you we've only got ten thousand dollars? And it's mostly in pledges."

"We can do it for five," Gerry said. "And if you can front a thousand or so, we can get started as soon as you want."

"How can you do it so cheap?" I wanted to know.

"Because most of it's ready to go—we did the same kind of thing last year up in San Francisco. Open air *Comedy of Errors.* We've still got the stage. All we have to do is knock it back together, anchor it and repaint it so it looks like what you want."

"Something else we could offer," Lou said. "We made some knock-down portable seats. Sort of like two-tier bleachers with backs. Seats about a thousand."

"Very good," Edmund said.

"And Fresnels. Will you be wanting Fresnels?" Lou said. "We've got those."

"Ah. Fresnels," Edmund said.

He knew nothing about lighting, I realized. All his plays in England had been done in sunlight. All our rehearsals so far had been done under bright work lights.

"Yes. We want you to light the show," I jumped in. "We'll run them if you can provide them."

"Provide 'em, set 'em up, run 'em if you want," Gerry said.

"An extra five hundred'll cover it," Lou said.

"Thanks," I said. "That'll be great."

Edmund gave me a grateful look. Then he extended his hand to Lou and Gerry. "Gentlemen, ye are hired," he said. "Now, we have an appointment with the management of this marketplace in thirty minutes. I suggest that we all go. It will give us cred."

The manager of Malpaso Row was a young well-dressed woman named Elizabeth Castillo. She wasn't used to offering part of her mall to theater types. But she also wasn't used to the level of charm that the three guys I was with knew how to project. Edmund was young, serious and full of passion. Every time she heard his British accent, she would smile. Lou was elegant. He talked a little about the sets he'd built, and leaned forward to listen every time Elizabeth Castillo had a question or a comment to make. And Gerry just threw out his legs, leaned back in his seat and smiled a testosterone-rich grin at her that never stopped.

In twenty minutes, the facilities manager leaned forward, gave all the guys a huge smile and said, "I wasn't inclined to say yes to your proposal, gentlemen, but I've changed my mind. Malpaso Row does have a policy of doing a certain amount of community outreach, and Shakespeare is popular. Taking everything into consideration, I think your play is an experiment that we can support."

And we walked out with permission to build a theater in the middle of a mall.

The four of us went to the bookstore next, and over an espresso, Edmund signed a contract with Lou and Gerry.

"You spoke of a thousand," Edmund said. "But I have two upon me, and ye may as well have them both now."

He pulled a wad of hundreds out of his hip pocket and handed them over to Lou.

"I'm going to enjoy this job," Lou said.

Two thousand bucks. Just like that. I shook my head. Maybe God did want to get this show up and running.

Chapter Twenty-Six

Edmund reassembled the cast the next night, in our backyard. Mom had been glad to let us use it, and had even helped with some mysterious project involving huge amounts of typing and editing. There were some boxes full of paper on the patio. When I asked what they were, Edmund only winked and said, "Patience."

About a quarter of the cast wasn't there. Word was they were tired of the fights and tension. Even if there was a good chance that those things were over, they'd had enough. Mostly, these were the smaller parts, but you know how they say there are no small parts, only small actors? This time it wasn't true. Verona was decimated.

Vivian was there, which didn't exactly cheer me up. I'd really hoped she'd quit. She kept away from Edmund, though, and sat close to her mother.

Drew was one of the missing, and that was much worse. You can't do *Romeo and Juliet* without Mercutio. I left messages on his phone and at his mother's studio.

The rest of us were lounging around on the grass in our

newly beautified yard. We were willing, but confused. We knew what we wanted to do, but not how we were going to do it. We wanted Edmund to tell us.

He didn't let us down. Standing on an upturned planter, he threw out his arms.

"I thank all of ye for your loyalty to this play. We are in excellent condition. We miss many friends tonight, but some will be coming back when they see we are serious, and hear what we have done already. Others we may replace with actors who were not cast the first time. And I promise you, we have enough to do this play with those who are here right now. We do need a good rehearsal space. Drew and I are working on that and I may have good news for you in a night or two. In any case, the show will go on. If I can, I mean to perform the best *Romeo and Juliet* ever, and I mean for us to leave a light in people's souls that will shine for the rest of their lives."

A few of us laughed and clapped.

"Beginning tonight, I want to start doing this show the way I've known it done in England," Edmund went on. "I have seen it work there, and it will work this time. From now on, if someone has a thought about how to make a scene better, speak up. You'll be amazed at what can happen."

Bill London put up his hand. "Edmund, I like the sound of what you're saying. But we're not professionals the way you are. We don't live this stuff. We need someone to tell us what to do."

Edmund nodded. "I take your point. But what I say is, let's do this play as I've known it done in England, where everyone can contribute what they think."

"But who decides?" Maria said. "Someone must decide."

"Come on, Ed," Bobby shouted. "If it weren't for you

we'd all be sitting around feeling sorry for ourselves. Take some responsibility, damn it. Be the director."

A lot of people shouted that Bobby was right.

"Okay, okay," Edmund said. "You all make sense. But I say we English know best how to mount a play, and this is the best way. When you have your new scripts in your hands you'll begin to see how this can work."

"New scripts?" I said. I had the script in my hip pocket. Unless Edmund's brother had done a total rewrite and sent it forward from 1597, I didn't need a new script.

"New scripts," Edmund said. "English-style scripts. We call them sides. And when you have your sides, you'll find this is a different play from what you've known so far."

Edmund began to hand out the contents of the boxes. Some of the scripts were only a few pages. Others were nearly the whole play. Each one had an actor's name at the top, together with their parts. And each script had nothing but that actor's cue lines and speeches. The rest of the play was gone.

"What's up with this?" Phil Hormel asked, looking up from his handful of sheets.

"It's how we did it in London the last time I was in this show," Edmund said. "I thought it might be interesting to try it. If it doesn't work out, we can always go back to the old way. But let's do act two this way and see what we get."

So we did.

And what we got was a whole new show.

I know, it was a new show anyway. But all of us had been in plays before, and none of us had done anything like this. It was a little like improv if you've ever done that, except that in improv you're making things up as you go along. Here, we were improvising to discover what was already there. But what was there changed as we did it.

At first, we were clumsy and slow. We missed cues, dropped lines. But then, like in improv where you have to concentrate on the other actors or you won't know what to do yourself, we learned to focus on everything the others were doing, and we started to fly.

Nobody was hanging around waiting for a cue. We didn't dare. We didn't want to. We knew we'd miss something. So we were not only a cast, we were an audience. And as the night went on, we got more and more into it and everything became more and more intense.

We still didn't finish that night. How could we when we kept coming up with questions and ideas and interrupting ourselves? But when ten o'clock came and it was time to pack it in, we kept on for another hour, and didn't want to stop then.

But we did, and then we applauded ourselves. We hugged. We jumped. We slapped each other's butts.

Bobby was so happy he couldn't even talk. He just punched the air over his head and squeaked.

Phil Hormel hugged himself.

Maria smiled like she really meant it.

And Vivian had a grim, but satisfied look on her face.

As for me, I was sure I could feel Edmund's iron resolve not to kiss Miranda ever again rusting away in my arms each time Romeo and Juliet clinched. This guy was mine, even if we'd only kissed once. Juliet just had to be patient.

Oh, did I mention that Edmund was brilliant? He was totally in charge and totally not throwing his weight around. He was Oberon the fairy king and we were his loyal sprites, and we were loving every minute of it. It was glorious, we were glorious and nobody wanted this night to end.

But end it did. People started to leave, and they were happy and excited, more than they'd been since the first night of rehearsals. I had a feeling that when word got around a lot of missing faces were going to be coming back.

I leaned back against a tree and watched the yard empty out.

"Helen of Troy thinks you did great tonight," I told Edmund.

"Ah. Yes. Well, ye see it does work..."

He was nervous. It was sweet.

Bobby was wandering around the yard, muttering lines and waving his arms, trying different things, in a world of his own. He didn't want to let go of this night any more than I did.

Drew came around the side of the house. Someone was with him, but I couldn't tell who it was.

"Dude. You're late," Bobby said.

"Where the hell have you been?" I asked.

Drew ignored us. "Excuse me, Edmund," he said. "This probably isn't the best time, but it's important. I mean, I didn't intend for this to happen, but we need—you need—to know about it right now."

I had never seen Drew like this. He was totally rattled.

"Drew, whatever it is, 'tis all well," Edmund assured him. "For the play will be well. And what beyond that can be wrong?"

"I'm not sure," Drew said.

"What is it, then?" Edmund asked.

Drew sighed. "There's someone with me I think you need to meet."

A tall man stepped into the patch of light coming from one of the back windows. I recognized him even though I'd never met him before.

That face. That bad portrait that Edmund had laughed at, was known all over the world. And now the living man was standing in my backyard next to Drew Jenkins, taking in everything he saw with the most beautiful eyes I'd ever seen.

"Give ye good evening, brother," said William Shakespeare.

Chapter Twenty-Seven

The Shakespeare boys did not seem all that glad to see each other. No hugs, no smiles. They stood apart. Edmund was tense as a taut guitar string. His big brother glowed with his sense of his own superiority.

"Give ye good evening, Will," Edmund said, making an elaborate bow, and looking at his brother like he was a pile of unwashed dishes. "How come ye here?"

"Marry, Doctor Dee did send me," William Shakespeare said. Then he bowed, not to Edmund, but to me. "Have I the honor of addressing the Lady Miranda?"

"I'm Miranda Hoberman."

"O, fairest of Juliets, of ye has Doctor Jenkins also spoken. I am honored to meet ye."

"And this is my friend Bobby Ruspoli," Drew said to Shakespeare.

"Give ye good evening, fair youth."

"Dude. This is major," Bobby said. "You brought da *Man.*" I'd never seen Bobby look so amazed, not even when he found out who Edmund really was. Then he bowed to Shakespeare.

Our new guest smiled, but Edmund didn't. His whole body was rigid with anger.

"Drew, my friend," he said. "What does this mean?"

"I–I was working on an idea I had..." Drew stuttered.

"Aye, indeed," Shakespeare interrupted. "Three messages has John Dee had of Doctor Jenkins. Three shining gems of intellect which he has shared with me. He treasures every word as if 'twere Holy Writ."

"But Drew, why told ye me nothing of this?" Edmund said.

"I wasn't expecting this to happen," Drew said. "I had an idea I was working on, and I was going to tell you as soon as I knew I had everything right—I mean, it could be dangerous. I didn't want anybody risking their life or disappearing besides me. And if it didn't work, I didn't want to disappoint you. But this—I didn't plan on it"

"Disappoint me? How?" Edmund said.

"My ultimate goal was to give you a way to go home. If you wanted to," Drew said.

"Ah," Edmund said slowly.

I thought back to that night when Drew had asked me what he could do for me, and I'd said, "Find a way to send an English lout back to his own time." Or something like that. And now Shakespeare was here. *The* Shakespeare. Not in London, not in the Renaissance where he belonged. In my backyard. I couldn't think. My brain was numb.

But I tried. "What…?" I said.

Drew seemed to understand what I was trying to say, sort of. "It—it isn't—frankly, I don't get—everything...." he said.

"Tell what ye can," Edmund said.

Drew let out a big breath. "Do you remember when you said that the theater was a metaphor for life?"

"Aye, for so it is," Edmund said.

"And, Miri, do you remember when your mom said maybe Doctor Dee had touched some kind of subatomic synchronicity or something, and you had possibly tapped into it for a second?"

"Yes. Get to the point, Drew. Quickly."

"Well that got me to thinking about how the Elizabethans used their stage. No fourth wall. No naturalism. The stage was wherever they needed it to be at that moment, especially the big area down front. We call it 'neutral space.'"

"We do call it 'the great,'" Shakespeare said. "'Play this on the great,' we say."

"So anyway, I thought that, if the stage is the world, then the world is a stage," Drew said.

"All the world's a stage!" Shakespeare said. *"All the men and women merely players.* I must write that down. Prithee, Doctor Jenkins, help me to recall it when I have a pen about me."

"I mean," Drew went on, "if one side of an equation equals something, then the other side equals the first. So the question then became, how do you create neutral space in the world? And if you can do that, is that the same thing as synchronicity? Because if it is, and all time is touching every other instant of time, then isn't it possible to move around in time and go where you want?"

"Brilliant," Shakespeare said. "Doctor Dee did dance me about his rooms when he read those words. And he's far too old for dancing. But tell now the best. Tell them of the paradox."

"Well, I didn't get very far with any of that until I remembered Zeno's First Paradox," Drew said.

"Zeno's paradox? 'Tis but a bauble of the mind," Edmund said.

"A jewel of the mind, ye mean, brother," Shakespeare said. "Listen on."

"Okay, for the benefit of all those of us who aren't geniuses?" Bobby said.

"Yeah, okay, right, sorry," Drew said. "Zeno's First Paradox is just a mind game, like Edmund said. Say Achilles and a turtle decide to have a race. To make things fairer, Achilles gives the turtle a head start. Off goes the turtle. Then Achilles starts. But the thing is, before he can catch up to the turtle, he's got to reach the halfway point to it. And the turtle is still moving. So, Achilles can never reach that halfway point. So he can never catch the turtle."

"That's stupid," Bobby said. "Of course he'll catch up to it."

"Right. Except that he can't, logically," Drew said. "That's the point. So anyway, I thought, maybe if I wrote a program that was based on the paradox, I could confuse time and create neutral space in cyberspace. I mean, cyberspace *is* neutral space, nearly. Then, maybe I could send an email to John Dee."

"Uhm, Drew. It's *1597* where he is," I said. "No computer. No electricity."

"Of course they had electricity," Drew said. "Electricity's been around forever. They just couldn't use it. I just had to hope Doctor Dee was doing something I could interface with."

"So how did Doctor Dee get your message?" Edmund asked.

"That was most wond'rous," Shakespeare said. "Doctor Dee has constructed a device of mercury and sulphur fumes in which bath most delicate copper letters do hang. It was his hope that he might conjure demons invisible to tell him where Edmund had gone. At midnight, in the dark of the moon, he did begin his first experiment. And as he watched, so he told me later, the copper alphabet began to tremble most visibly. Words did come, one after the other. At first he could not credit it. But then he wrote down what he had seen and showed me this the next day."

Shakespeare pulled out a piece of parchment from his doublet and handed it to Edmund. I looked over his shoulder. In the light from the windows, I read.

Doctor John Dee,
My name is Drew Jenkins. I am living in America in the early twenty-first century, and I am trying to contact you to tell you what has happened to Edmund Shakespeare or Shakeshaft. He is here with us, alive, well and acting in his brother's play *Romeo and Juliet*. I can't be sure how he came here, but I think it had something to do with the momentary creation of what you might call neutral space. In any case, if you see William Shakespeare, please tell him that his brother is fine and that I am working to make it possible for him to come home, if he wants to.
Best Regards,
Drew Jenkins

"Doctor Dee was beside himself with joy and excitement," Shakespeare said. "But there was naught to do but to tell me the great news and to wait, hoping that Doctor Jenkins would try again to pierce the veil of time."

Drew was looking a touch more relaxed, but I couldn't calm down myself. "My next email was a lot longer. Pages long, in fact. I thought that if I told Doctor Dee as much as

I could about what I was doing and what my equipment was like, he might be able to come up with a way to contact me. And he did."

"Doctor Dee did concoct a lightning bath, using lore which Doctor Jenkins sent," Shakespeare said. "Then, using it to increase the virtue of the device which he already had, he used the copper alphabet to scribe on time itself."

"He means I sent the technology for the wet-cell battery," Drew said. He shrugged like it was nothing. "It's simple, really. The Babylonians probably had them. But all the rest was Doctor Dee's. Anyway, I got a message back, but it took me a few days to discover it. It went into my spam file. Mostly it was questions about the future. But he also mentioned that Will—that Master Shakespeare here—wanted to know everything about what Edmund was doing. So I told him about the play. Then today, when I started to write to Doctor Dee again, there was this low throbbing, kind of like an earthquake, and a bright light, and—"

"And I did come into this wond'rous world like a being newly born," Shakespeare said. "I was with Doctor Dee standing in his sanctum sanctorum as he tried to send another message to Doctor Jenkins when I did feel myself enraptured by a force unknowable and translated in all time and no time to stand beside great Doctor Jenkins."

"Ye mean, *brother,* ye thought to throw yourself into Doctor Dee's pentagram to see if ye might come here and admire your own greatness," Edmund sneered.

"I have always been a brave man."

Now that I was past the initial shock of seeing William Shakespeare in my backyard, my brain was jumping around like an excited puppy. Edmund's big brother was here. Where were we going to put him? How were we going to fit him into this world? Was he truly as vain as he seemed to be? And what was going to happen to English literature now that he wasn't in his own time to write the rest of his plays?

"Drew, who else knows Shakespeare is here?" I asked.

"No one, fortunately. I got us out of the house before my mom came home. So we've just been driving around. It seemed like the best thing to do."

"Doctor Jenkins has shown me marvels," Shakespeare said. "We have ridden about in his thunder cart, and he has driven me through the place where the play will be acted. A fine site, I think."

This was awful. We now had two Renaissance Englishmen to try to hide. Two who obviously didn't like each other. Who couldn't bunk together, unless we *wanted* to end up with a debt-of-honor duel or something. Where were we going to put this new Shakespeare?

My brain stopped jumping around and landed on one great fact.

"Drew," I said. "He has to go home. You have to get him back."

"Aye," Edmund said. "And that soon."

"Now, brother," Shakespeare purred. "A man might almost think his kin wasn't glad to see him."

"You don't understand, sir," I said. "If Edmund slips out of your world and into ours, it's not a big deal. But you're famous. If you disappear from history—well, it won't be good for history."

"Famous," Shakespeare said. "Yes. Doctor Jenkins did mention that in his letters. I should like to know more about that when time is convenient."

"What are you going to do about this?" I said to Drew.

"I don't know.... But there must be an equation in there someplace."

"And no doubt in God's good time Doctors Dee and Jenkins will find it," Shakespeare said. "And my brother and I will go home."

"Nay, Will. I will never go back to England," Edmund emphatically proclaimed. "I will stay and become an actor here such I could never be in England."

"Let that be as it must be," Shakespeare shrugged. "But in the meantime, there is another matter I wish to discuss. Since I am here, I wish to help my brother to perform my play."

"All the parts are given out," Edmund said.

"'Tis *Romeo and Juliet,*" Shakespeare said. "There is always room for another citizen of Verona."

"Not for thee," Edmund said.

"Wretch! Then I forbid ye to perform it."

"Forbid? Who are ye to forbid?" Edmund questioned. "Think ye that the Lord Chancellor will help ye to prevent it? The Master of the Revels close the theaters for ye? Be damned to ye, Will Shakespeare. The play will go on."

"Brother, I ask only—" Shakespeare began.

"Ye ask only to snivel yer way onto the stage and take it over! I know your little ways, Will. There is no part for ye."

"Edmund, ye little bastard, ye've no more right to prevent me being in me own play than ye have to steal the part of Romeo," Shakespeare roared.

"Steal? I was parted for my skill," Edmund roared back. "We real actors must earn our way on our abilities."

"Look, guys. We can settle this," Bobby was saying. "There's no point in anybody getting hysterical."

But the Shakespeare brothers weren't listening. They were busy getting hysterical.

"Ye will never set foot on our stage," Edmund shouted.

To which Shakespeare responded by slapping Edmund across the face and spitting on him.

To which Edmund responded by launching himself at his brother.

In the next second they were down on the grass wrestling and punching. And it was nothing like the fight that Drew and Bobby had had. This was a nasty, tear-your-clothes and kick-you-in-the-eye fight with the most amazing exotic curses I'd ever heard, erupting out of both their handsome mouths.

The back door opened.

"What the hell is going on?" Mom said.

Her voice rang with power. Maybe Queen Elizabeth had sounded like that. If not, she would have given her orb and scepter to be able to do it.

Shakespeare, who was on top of Edmund, looked up. Edmund turned his head toward Mom.

Mom took a step down from the door, which made the light behind her shine full on Shakespeare's face.

"Mom, this is Edmund's brother, Will..."

"Yes...I can see that," she said in a very quiet voice. She leaned against the door frame. Her face was full of amazement.

Then, it changed. I saw it set into that tough, determined look she had when she'd come to a decision.

"Everybody inside," she said. "We'll sort this out."

Chapter Twenty-Eight

And Mom did. When she had found out everything that had happened, she became very practical, as perhaps only a mom can be when faced with brawling Elizabethan time travelers. Shakespeare would sleep on the couch in the living room. Before that, he would take a shower—although, I noticed, Shakespeare didn't have the incredible stink that Edmund had brought with him—he reeked of stale perfumes instead. Then he would dress in some more of my dad's old clothes.

Then Mom thought for a while. We all waited for her to lay down the law to everybody.

"Edmund, your brother's in the show," she said in her take-charge nurse voice. "As long as he's here, we might as well get some use out of him. Mister Shakespeare, you will accept any part you are given, and you will do everything you can to help your brother. Drew Jenkins, you will stop contacting Doctor Dee until and unless I give you permission. Do you all understand me?"

"But, Ms. Hoberman, if I don't contact Doctor Dee—" Drew began.

"You are in over your head!" Mom barked suddenly, but then regained her composure. "Drew, I appreciate that you were trying to help Edmund. But I have to point out that you've failed to do that. And you have made things a lot more complicated. You've performed major surgery on the past. So we're going to see how the patient does before we do anything more. Got it?"

"Got it," Drew said, and nodded.

"And are you both clear on the play?" Mom asked Edmund and his brother.

"I like it not, milady, but 'twill be so," Edmund said.

"Ye are wise as ye are beautiful," Shakespeare said. "I repent me that I had to meet ye in such wise as I did. My brother did provoke me."

Edmund opened his mouth. I put out my hand and touched his arm. His mouth closed again.

"Thank you." Mom smiled. "In spite of all the difficulties your presence here raises, it's an honor beyond telling to meet you, Master Shakespeare. Just one thing."

"Aye, milady?" Shakespeare said.

"You seem to be a vain man. Vain, and ambitious. Edmund is a friend of mine. If you do anything to try to undermine his control of the play—if you put a foot wrong in any way—I'll cut that foot off. And I'm a trained nurse. I know just where to cut, Mister Shakespeare. Welcome to California."

Shakespeare looked very thoughtful. "Brother, d'ye not think her much like our sister Joan?" he said at last.

"Aye, as our Joan might be had she had such chances to be learned as Milady Hoberman has had," Edmund agreed.

"Our sister Joan is a great woman," Shakespeare said. "I will swear to you, milady, as I would swear to her, that I will be loyal. Whatever service I can do, that I will, and no more. 'Twill be enough to see how my play is done in these marvelous times. I have but one more request."

"And that would be?" Edmund said.

"Doctor Jenkins has spoken of a folio," Shakespeare said.

"Ah. No wonder ye came to the twenty-first century," Edmund said. "Now ye can steal lines from yourself."

"I'll get it," I said.

But when I went to the coffee table where Edmund had left it, it was gone. And it wasn't in its place on the shelf. It wasn't anywhere.

So we all went looking for it, anyplace we thought it might be, until Drew slapped his forehead and said, "Idiot!"

"What?" I said.

"There is no First Folio. Shakespeare's here, so the plays were never collected."

"Wait, wait. Then how come we all know it exists?" Mom said. "Shouldn't we have no memory of it if it doesn't exist?"

"No," Drew said. "Because it did exist until this afternoon. We all remember it. But right now there isn't a single First Folio, or Second Folio, or Third Folio or *Riverside Shakespeare* anywhere in the world."

"Whoa," Bobby said. "That's big."

"Damn it," Shakespeare said. "To come so far and find my coming has all but erased my reputation—but how is it then that *Romeo and Juliet* still is known?"

"Written before you disappeared," Mom said.

"Would you like to look yourself up?" Drew said.

"What?" Shakespeare said.

"Take a look at what is still known about you?" Drew explained.

"Aye," Shakespeare said. "That I would."

Drew went out to his car and came back with his computer. He flipped it open and the screen glowed. The screen saver came on, random shapes and colors moving in an endless pattern.

Shakespeare gasped.

"'Tis beautiful," he said.

"Okay," Drew said quietly. "Let's see what kind of a world we're living in without that book."

He typed in "William Shakespeare."

There were quite a few entries, and they all said pretty much the same thing. Here's one.

Shakespeare, William (1564–1597?) English poet and playwright. Shakespeare was a prominent writer of the English Renaissance best known for his long poem *Venus and Adonis,* and three plays, *Richard III, Henry V* and *Romeo and Juliet,* which are still sometimes performed. He is known to have been born in Stratford-on-Avon, probably on April 23rd 1564. The date of his death is not known, but no mention of him occurs after 1597. Many scholars consider that he had not come into the fullness of his powers, and that had he lived his best work might well have awaited him.

That was all.

"Three plays?" Shakespeare said. "I have written a dozen."

"No one collected them," Drew said. "Only the most popular ones survived."

"Mom," I said in a panic. "You still used to be an actress, right?"

"Sure," she said.

"Did you ever work three seasons in Ashland at the Shakespeare Festival?"

"The what?" she said. Then a look of horror crossed her face. "Oh, God... I did do that. But at the same time, I know there's no Shakespeare Festival there now. And there's no Globe Theater in San Diego."

"This is getting out of control," I said.

"Word," Bobby said.

"Yea, verily," I agreed.

"Hah," Edmund said. "Undone by your own vanity, Will."

"You behave. Now is not the time to gloat," Mom said.

The phone rang.

"I'd better get it," I said. "Maybe Doctor Dee has invented the telephone."

I went to the kitchen and picked up the receiver.

From far away, I heard Dad's voice. "Hello, Miri, it's your father."

My who? I thought crazily. On top of everything else that had happened tonight, this phone call was almost too much to take in. Then a wave of total happiness crashed over me.

Chapter Twenty-Nine

"Daddy?" I eeped.

"Yes, honey," Dad said. "It's me. Did I wake you?"

"No," I said. "Daddy—are you coming home?'

"That's what I'm calling about," Dad said. "Can I speak to my wife? And to you?"

"Okay, yes," I said. "I'll go get her."

When I told her, Mom walked to the phone. But I knew she wanted to run.

Our first words were tentative, a little clumsy. But Dad's voice was like a golden river pouring into my ears, into my heart. And when he and Mom spoke, I could hear the love between them.

"I've called to ask if I can come home," Dad said.

"Yes," Mom said. "What's the next question?"

"There isn't one," Dad said.

"Then get on back here," I blurted out.

Mom laughed.

"Yes. If you'll have me. I'll start tomorrow."

Then we all just listened to each other breathing for a minute.

"You probably want to know why I'm calling in the middle of the night to ask to come back," Dad said finally.

"Not especially," Mom said. "It's not important. What's important is that you're coming."

"I think I need to tell you anyway," Dad said. "I've wanted to ask that question for a long time now. But I couldn't do it, because all my searching for myself had really only led me to one conclusion. That I was a selfish jerk ever to have left you. And that raised the question of whether you weren't better off without me. I had a good job now, working as a shrink again. Maybe I should just send money and keep out of your lives. So I decided to wait for some kind of indicator of what to do."

Mom didn't say anything. Neither did I.

"Then tonight I had a dream that seemed to answer the question for me," he went on. "You know how I use dreams in my work with my clients. Well, this one felt as important as any I've ever had or heard of. Not my usual kind of thing. May I tell you?"

"Go on," Mom said.

"I was staring into a pot of water looking at my own reflection. Then my face changed into the face of a woman. She was wearing some kind of old-fashioned cap and she looked strong, noble. She had a long nose, and dark eyes, and she said, 'Return, fool, to the place ye once called home. Your work is there.' Then her face went away and I saw an old man with a long white beard. He said, 'Portentous and perilous is the state of the work. Shakespeare dwells where you should be. Go and tell him—' and that's when I woke up. About two hours ago. And I've been lying here ever since trying to work the dream out in terms of my anima and my archetypal old man. That's clear enough. And the Shakespeare reference obviously refers to both of you as actresses. But the intensity of the dream is what's so significant. It was like I wasn't sleeping at all. Those two people felt absolutely real—"

"You'd better tell him what's going on, Miri," Mom said.

And I did.

When I was done, Dad was so amazed he could hardly speak. "I can't—" he began. Then, "How on earth—?" Then, "Do you think I can be of any use? Never mind. I'm coming. I'm coming home. Shakespeare. My God."

"Miri," Mom said. "Your father and I need some time to talk."

"I'll go check on the guys," I said.

The four of them were lying on the furniture in the living room asleep or half-asleep. They raised their heads when I came in.

"My dad's coming home," I said.

"Then I shall meet the great doctor of souls!" Edmund said. "Excellent!"

"Yeah, pretty excellent." I threw my arms around Edmund, loving him, feeling him wanting to love me back. Then, when he'd disentangled himself—reluctantly, I thought—I hugged Drew like the friend he was.

"Thank you, Drew," I said. "If you hadn't started fooling around with Achilles and his turtle, this wouldn't be happening."

"Really?"

I told him about Dad's dream, and about Joan Hart's scrying.

"Wow," Bobby said. "Friend Drew, thou art a mighty geek."

Drew shook his head. "I'm glad your dad is coming home,

Miri. I'm glad for anything I did to help. But this is serious. If Joan Hart can scry your dad, and Doctor Dee can see him, too—that implies that something's up with whatever it is that separates our time from theirs. More than I realized. Your mom was right. I am in *way* over my head."

He looked so worried that I moved over and sat beside him on the sofa and hugged him again. "Drew, it's okay. You meant well. It's not your fault if the time flow or whatever starts backing up like a clogged toilet."

"What did Doctor Dee say in your father's dream?" Drew said. "Something about perils and portents? Perils doesn't sound good.... I sent the plans for wet-cell technology! Doctor Dee made a battery following them."

"Yeah, and if you hadn't he wouldn't have been able to answer your messages, right?" Bobby asked, confused.

"Yes. But then William Shakespeare showed up in my room today," Drew went on. "And I wasn't even trying to do that. To bring him here. See what I mean? Equation. I send something there, so something from there has to come here. But it's not an exact equation, which suggests that there's some kind of balance that's out of balance—"

"Oh, my God," I said. "Does that mean somebody from our time ended up in Edmunds' time when he came here?"

"If I'm right, then, yes," Drew said. "But we're probably never going to know."

Drew's phone buzzed.

"No, Mom, I'm fine," he said into it. "I'm at Miri's with some of the cast. Two in the morning, I know. Yes, of course, sorry. Be there in fifteen."

He put the phone away.

"Are you in trouble?" I asked him.

"I suppose that depends on how you define trouble," he said. "On the one hand, my mom's a little angry with me, and it's so late I'm going to be dead on my feet at work tomorrow. On the other hand, I may have started the unraveling of time....which seems somehow worse."

Edmund and Shakespeare looked solemn. Drew, hunched on the sofa, looked like he felt completely alone.

Bobby tugged on Drew's arm.

"Come on, man. You'll figure it out. Or Doctor Dee will. But you gotta get some sleep. If you don't you'll go crazy."

Drew got up. "If I'm not crazy already. I'm not sure. See you tomorrow, guys. Later today, I mean. See—can't tell yesterday from today, time problems, ha ha. Anyway, thanks for the hugs."

"Here. Have another," I said, and hugged him again. "It's good to have you for a friend, Drew."

"Yeah. You, too, Miri. Good night."

The door closed behind him and I wondered what it would be like to have a brain like that, to live in a world like his. I wondered if that very special brain had anything to do with why I never saw him with a girl.

Chapter Thirty

Dad was coming home. Everything was going to be good again. I couldn't wait; the three days it was going to take him to get to us seemed like three hundred years. I'd have gone crazy if I hadn't had the show to do.

Drew's mom was able to get us the use of the parish hall at St. Stephen's, the church where she preached sometimes, for our rehearsals. St. Stephen's was an old church built in a kind of medieval style and the hall went well with the show.

Then there was Shakespeare.

When Edmund introduced him, he said, "Everyone, this is my brother Bill. He just got here from England. He thinks he can act. I told him he could take over a couple of small parts. So if he tries to give you any advice about how to do your lines—Don't. Listen. To. Him."

We all laughed. Including Shakespeare.

And the Bard behaved himself. The casual arrogance I'd picked up on the night he arrived was gone. Maybe giving him a show to be in improved his character. He was quiet during breaks, and polite to everyone, even his brother. But he was so good, even in the small parts he was given, that he made the rest of us see how we could do our own roles better. And when we broke for discussions about how to improve a scene or a line, and what it really meant, the one guy on the planet who could have let us know exactly what the author intended stood back and stroked his beard, maybe asking a question or two. And always a good question that led to the best answer for that actor.

Nobody recognized him the way we had. Why would they? In Dad's clothes, with his hair pulled back in a ponytail, he looked like a middle-age guy doing community theater. After rehearsals, Edmund, Bobby, Shakespeare, Drew and I crowded into Drew's car and came back to our place. We sat around with Mom, talking about the show until way after midnight.

There was still tension between the brothers, and it could blow up away from the theater. The first night after rehearsal, Shakespeare said to Bobby, "I like well your Tybalt. Ye bring something to the role I have not seen before. I think it is a secret good-heartedness. I did not write it so, but 'tis charming."

"Wow, Will," Bobby said. "Coming from you, that means everything."

But the remark made Edmund snap. "Will, damn ye—ye gave your word. Do not be gulled by him, Bobby. He likes your playing little and wants ye to change it. 'Tis his way to charm when he cannot command. Next will come a few modest suggestions which ye will be a fool to take."

"I meant no more than I said," Shakespeare said. "What a rogue ye must think me."

"Aye, I do. For ye are," Edmund said.

And Bobby looked hurt.

But then in a few minutes we were back to the flow of

good talk, and after a while, Edmund said, "At least what my brother told ye is true, Bobby. Your Tybalt is something new."

When it was over and Drew and Bobby went home, I thought, *This is what my life is going to be like. Love, and Shakespeare, and acting and theater twenty-four-seven forever. And my dad is coming home.*

And on Saturday, Dad drove up in an ancient Toyota crammed with his stuff.

When I heard a car door slam, I ran to the living-room window—not like I'd been waiting or anything—and I called out, "He's here."

Mom came in from the kitchen.

Edmund and Will had been waiting with me. Edmund stood up.

"Come, brother. Let us absent ourselves from their felicity awhile."

Shakespeare stood up and followed him down the hall murmuring, "Absent—felicity..."

Which meant he was trying to remember it until he could write it down.

I opened the door. There Dad stood, weary, tall and long faced, looking more like a wet dog than anything else. Seeing him again, so familiar, and so strange, was almost like recognizing Shakespeare had been. But Dad's portrait was in my heart. It would change to fit this slightly different face.

"Miri," he said.

"Daddy," I said.

"I love you," he said, and embraced me.

And then Mom was there, standing beside me, running one hand through her long ash-blond hair, a little off-balance and looking up at him.

I took a step out of Dad's arms.

"Ohhh," Dad said and wrapped himself around his wife.

They stood there a long time, holding each other and breathing things that made me want to say, "Hey, guys, get a room."

So I went and knocked on Edmund's door.

"Let me in," I said. "Mom and Dad need privacy, and so do I."

"You are come in very good time," Shakespeare said. "I am seized with an idea for a play. And there is a part in it for you."

He had a pile of paper in front of him covered with his old-fashioned scrawl in blue ballpoint ink.

"'Tis a piece of old trash he is rewriting," Edmund said.

"'Twill not be trash when I have worked it over."

"What do you call it?" I asked.

"*The Tragedy of Hamlet, Prince of Denmark,* I think," Shakespeare said.

"A fig on it," Edmund said. "Everyone has seen the old one."

"No, no, don't knock it," I said. "He may be on to something."

And that afternoon in our spare bedroom, I read some of Ophelia's lines as they came from Will Shakespeare's hand. And when Mom finally knocked on our door and said thank you and we could come out now, there was almost half of the first act.

The Shakespeare brothers entered the living room graceful and elegant in Dad's polo shirts and jeans. Together, they bowed to him. Dad offered his hand.

"Gentlemen, call me Paul," he said.

"We give thanks, sir, for your gracious welcome," Shakespeare said.

Edmund took Dad's hand and said, "Tell us, Doctor, for my brother and I are most interested, what is this psychology ye do?"

"Ah," Dad said. He stood up straight like he'd just forgotten he was tired. And by the time Dad had finished answering him about four hours later, the Shakespeares had heard all about Freud, Jung, Adler, gestalt, archetypes, repression, suppression, the collective unconscious, the id, the ego and a few hundred other things.

Dad asked them a million questions about England, what they dreamed about, and had their dreams changed since they came here, and what had that been like, flying through time from Doctor Dee's secret chambers to our kitchen, and to Drew's room.

They were at it until midnight while Mom and I watched and smiled at our guys, as excited with each other as if they'd discovered buried treasure.

The next day, Dad started having counseling sessions with the Shakespeares. It was their idea.

"If it can be that my brother and I may be better friends—" Shakespeare said at breakfast.

"—or friends at all," Edmund said. "We would be so. Do ye think your psychology may make the world big enough for both of us?"

"I've seen much worse," Dad said, and took them into the room he used as an office.

Sessions like that are supposed to be private, of course. The thing was, the Shakespeares wouldn't stop talking. Wherever they were, whatever else we were doing—except for the show—they were rehashing everything they didn't like about each other.

For instance, Edmund hated the way Will was always quoting him in his plays.

"Ye are a thief," Edmund shouted one afternoon. "A jackdaw rogue who hasn't an idea or a word in his head that someone else didn't put there. As I know better than most."

"Thief? I do but take in all that crosses my path, a thing I can no more change than the color of my skin. And I give back all, transformed!"

"Bah."

"And by the bye, your acting is not near as good as you want the world to think," Will said.

"Okay," Dad said. "We're getting somewhere."

And somehow or other, they were. Dad could always ask the questions that took the brothers deep into their words to find the feelings that lay buried beneath them.

And because they were both actors and both brilliant and both Shakespeares, they were moving fast. It was only a few days before Edmund shouted out, "I know what 'tis, Will—"

And before he could finish, Shakespeare answered, "'Tis that we are too much alike!"

And they laughed long and hard.

"Ye will always be a rogue and a scoundrel," Edmund said.

"And ye will always wish to be more of one," Shakespeare said.

"We're making progress," Dad concluded.

It was a crazy time. Drew and Bobby were in and out, Mom and Dad were reconnecting. There was so much going on at once that I could feel my life flying toward something new. My life was changing, finding a new pattern, moving forward to something I wasn't sure of, but knew I wanted. You could say it was chaotic—but in a good way. The old Mom, Dad and Miri dynamic that Dad had walked out on was only a memory—but memory is very important stuff. But each of us was working toward this new family idea which seemed to fall naturally on all of us as soon as Dad hit the door.

As for Edmund and me, we were together every night, but always in the middle of a crowd. It wasn't perfect—I definitely wanted to hear more of what we'd been talking about that day when Mom had come home so inconveniently—but on the other hand, we were in each other's arms every night, with his brother's words to say to each other, and we meant every one of them.

And Dad didn't have any more dreams about Joan Hart or Doctor Dee. It gave me hope that the past was starting to heal up, as Mom had thought it might. I was sure Shakespeare would get back to England eventually, somehow, and Edmund would stay. And we would be together.

Chapter Thirty-One

The play was taking on its shape. We were all getting better.

Phil Hormel had been playing Friar Lawrence as a goody-goody. It's easy to do it that way—I mean, he's a friar, right? And he speaks in couplets and talks about flowers. But what kind of goody-goody knows so much about poisons and knockout drugs? So Friar Lawrence has something about him that isn't quite in focus, like maybe being a friar had been a career change and before that he'd been something else, like a professional assassin. Edmund helped him to see this, and to act it. And Phil was good.

Bill Meisinger was becoming less of a mellow-voiced stick. Ann Millard was relying less on playing the nurse for laughs and finding her way toward the real character—a loving old woman. I had to admit, even Vivian was beginning to shine. She found things to do in the party scene, on the streets of Verona, and even in the role where she had to play a really stupid servant with a message to deliver—and a boy servant at that, so none of her sexiness was useful there.

As for me, I got what was probably the ultimate compliment from the author. "Your Juliet is most believable," he told me one night. "I do not think any boy could play it better."

Things were getting busy behind the scenes, too. Tanya Blair was drowning in work, trying to get the tickets printed and some publicity done. And, since no one was in charge of costumes, she had those on her, as well. When she heard about it, Mom stepped in to help, dragging Dad with her.

"It's not like you have any paying clients right now," she told him. "You might as well make yourself useful."

To keep costs down, we all dressed in rehearsal clothes, with something red for the Capulets and something blue for the Montagues. Almost the only things we needed to rent were the swords.

Edmund was completely happy with that.

"In London we most often provide our own costumes," he told me. "Piece them out with such weapons and bits of armor as we have in store. It works well."

Tickets, on the other hand, were a complete surprise.

"Tickets?" Edmund said when I told him, like it was the first time he'd heard the word, which as it turned out, it was.

"Playgoers give a penny or two at the theater door," Shakespeare said.

"No, no, no," I said. "Nowadays people pay for their seats in advance. They get little pieces of paper with the date and time and even their seat numbers on them. And they pay a lot more than a penny."

"We could pass a hat, perhaps," Edmund said.

"No," I said.

But it worked out, the same way everything was working out. Tanya Blair and my mom and dad got some printed, put up a website and sold them online and out of Drew's mom's yoga studio. And people bought them.

On the Wednesday before opening, our set started to go up. Gerry and Lou trucked it in at seven that morning, and by the time the stores closed that night, fair Verona where we lay our scene was looming over its fake Italian streets.

And it was beautiful. Much more elaborate than anything we had talked about. There were details like fake stonework around the doors and windows, and shields with the crests of the Montagues and Capulets hanging from two of the houses. Between the houses, helping to steady them, was an arch that worked as a central entrance, a street and, at the end of the play, the way to the Capulet tomb. There was a skull and crossbones on it throughout the play. Perfect.

All the actors walked around the set in awe that first night. We tried to look like we were being total pros, just figuring out how to inhabit this new space, not really overwhelmed at how beautiful it looked, and how much we hoped to shine in it. But we were blown away.

"We never throw anything away," Lou said when I told him how amazing it was.

"Hell, tell her the truth. We scrounge from other theaters," Gerry laughed. "As soon as they strike a set, we show up to rescue it from the Dumpsters. I'll bet we could stage four *Oklahoma!*'s at once."

"There's still some work to do," Lou said. "We have some banners and stuff. And the lights to move in."

"Even so," Edmund said. "You've done everything you said you'd do and more. I've never seen better, not even in England."

It would have been nice if there'd been some way to stop the looky-lous from stopping by for an eyeful of free theater. Shoppers walking up and down the mall saw what we were doing, and stopped and stared, surrounded by their bags, kids and dogs, blocking the streets, which made the drivers start honking their horns. Not something actors had had to deal with back in the 1590's.

"To be or not to be, is that the question?" some guy in a motorcycle T-shirt shouted at Edmund.

"Hey, Juliet, baby, over here," hollered a guy in a Raiders cap. "I'll be your Romeo."

It was hell. People were shouting at each other, shouting at us. Little kids were screaming. Two dogs started to fight.

After that night, Elizabeth Castillo came down from her office and told us we'd have to hire at least two extra security guards for every night we were in the mall.

"Two be damned," Edmund said. "How much for a dozen?"

"They're two hundred dollars a shift," Elizabeth Castillo said.

"Get me six, and I want them at once," Edmund said.

"Edmund, there's no way the show can make that kind of money," I said. "Not even if we sell out every night."

"A fig for the cost," Edmund raged. "We need those dogberries and we will have them."

Elizabeth Castillo put her hand over her mouth like there was something she was trying to keep herself from saying. Then she said it. "We'll cover the cost of one guard out of special-event funds."

"Bless ye, milady," Edmund said.

Elizabeth Castillo smiled. "Some nights we might be able to stretch it to two."

Things were better the next night, with our own pair of giants to keep people moving and quiet. Nothing like a three-hundred-pound weightlifter asking you to move along to make you want to do it.

And the trouble on that first night actually helped. A guy came down from the paper to find out more about it, and did a nice article on the show. It ended up on the first page of the local section, and a lot of people who hadn't known we were doing the play read it. They wanted tickets.

But the pedestrian problems were tiny compared with the lights. It was the only time I ever saw Edmund really upset with the way things were going.

Setting lights brought things to a crawl, starting and stopping while Gerry and Lou scrambled around on the rig of pipes and lines that they had rented to us and which, one by one, erased the unwanted shadows from the set. We were there past midnight three nights in a row because of all the work it made.

The whole lighting thing fascinated Shakespeare. As the Fresnels went up, he watched with the same amazing intensity that Edmund brought to whatever he wanted to know. When Gerry finally called down from a pole he was hanging on, "Hey, Bill, you wanta help?" Shakespeare almost flew up to where he was and started learning to aim and mask the lights. He was so happy he started whistling, and the work went a little faster at least.

Edmund still fumed.

"I swear, Miri, these damned lights will keep us from opening on time," he said. "Hell's cullions, they may keep us here till Doomsday waiting. No one needs them. We have the most glorious sun here in California. We can play in it, as they did in London."

"Look, Edmund," I said. "People don't go to the theater in the middle of the day anymore. They go at night. And believe me, light is worth all the trouble it takes. Wait and see."

"I like them well, brother," Shakespeare said. "Burbage owns an old church which we might light by candles and perform shows at night there. If I ever get home to England, I will talk him into it."

Thursday we had final dress rehearsal. And it went so well I was worried. Because you know that old saying that a bad dress rehearsal means a good opening night? It's usually true. There's something about having one last chance to make a bunch of mistakes that sets you up to do well the next time.

Anyway, we were going to find out. Opening night was Friday.

Chapter Thirty-Two

One of the worst things about being an actor is the day of opening night. You are worthless. You can't think about anything but getting onstage, and whether you're going to screw up in front of a thousand people. You try to avoid every other human being, because if anybody talks to you, they're almost certain to get snapped at, or ignored, at best.

Mom and Dad kept out of my way.

I could have worked with Edmund, but he wasn't there. He and Shakespeare had promised to help Gerry and Lou with some of the last setup items.

I tried to rehearse my part by myself, but that was just reciting, not acting.

Finally, when it was still an hour before my call, I headed down to the theater anyway, because there was nowhere else on earth for me to be.

And when I got to there, I stopped, gasped, smiled, cried. Because Gerry and Lou and the guys had been busy.

Lou had mentioned something about banners a week ago, and I hadn't really paid attention. But they were there now.

On one side of the mall hung red banners for the Montagues. On the other side, all around the area of the theater, were the blue banners of the Capulets. The expensive apartments and stores surrounding the stage had become part of the scene. I was in Verona.

And standing on an apartment balcony was Edmund. Side by side with Gerry and Lou, and, presumably, the nice woman who lived there. She was smiling happily. Gerry had his arm around her waist.

"Miri!" Edmund shouted when he saw me. "Come up."

"This'll be the first time Juliet ever climbed up to Romeo," I said, but I went into the building and took the elevator to the second floor.

"Hi, I'm Carol," the lady said, letting me in. "Isn't it amazing? You guys are amazing. Turning this whole place into something—something—I don't know. Amazing."

"Something rich and strange," Edmund said.

From Carol's balcony I could see both sides of the set, the beautiful façade and the strong, workmanlike backstage. The canvas-walled dressing rooms, and the short black tower where Gerry and Lou would run the lights. And the banners fluttered over it all.

"Thank you," I said, and slowly put my arms around Edmund, who had given me this.

"No, Miri. Thank you," Edmund said. Edmund looked down at me, and his face held that same look it had on the day when I'd knighted him at the kitchen sink. "Kind lady, gentle sirs, will ye not give me a moment alone with her in this place?"

"Whoa," Gerry said.

"Oh, how sweet," Carol said.

They left and Edmund closed the balcony door.

"Miri," he said. "Ye remember that day?"

"Yes," I said.

"So do I. I have not been able to fight down my feelings for ye," he said. "I have tried, but failed. Miri, will ye have my love and be my Juliet in life?"

"Aye. I will take you for my Romeo."

Edmund took me in his arms and kissed me, and from the other balconies and from the sidewalks below, came cheers.

"Break a leg," he whispered.

"Break a leg." I nodded.

And we went back into the apartment.

"'Tis well," Edmund told Gerry, Carol and Lou. "My love loves me, and we have a play to act."

Carol, Gerry and Lou applauded.

And with that, we went down to get ready.

The other actors began to arrive. Drew and Bobby, Maria and Vivian, Phil, Bill London and everyone else. They all seemed to be charged with some special beauty that shone out of their faces and made their movements full of meaning. There was a power in us that I'd never felt before on any opening night.

Which is not to say we felt that way about ourselves. We were scared.

Drew was pacing back and forth, whispering his lines, occasionally stabbing at the air with an empty hand. Bobby was in a corner, made up, coiled into himself. Vivian kept checking her face.

A low murmur that grew louder as we waited told us that the audience was arriving. The sun slanted down below the roofline of the apartments, and a breeze off the sea made the banners stream and fall so it looked like the show itself was breathing.

Bill Meisinger, dressed in a handsome black suit and gleaming shoes stood with his arms wrapped around himself, waiting in the wings. Beside him was Tanya Blair in plain black work clothes. She was carrying her faithful clipboard and wearing a headset. Total pro.

I saw her adjust the mike and whisper into it, nod. She touched Bill on his shoulder, strode out into the light and welcomed the audience.

She exited, and a couple of people actually applauded her. Then Gerry changed the lighting cue, and Bill walked out.

Now understand, Bill was an announcer. And always before he'd done his role by zeroing in on the center of the stage, announcing his lines and leaving the way he'd come in. And I would swear that that was exactly what he meant to do this time. But somehow, when the lights hit him, he changed.

He walked along the set upstage, not strolling, but leading the audience. He had something important to show us as well as to say. His arm shot up, pointing to the Capulet banner.

"*Two* households, both alike in dignity,
In fair Verona where we lay our scene,
From ancient grudge break to *new* mutiny...."

He wasn't announcing, he was telling us a story, a story that mattered hugely. And the actors standing backstage heard his words fresh and full of new meaning, and were gathered in.

He cast a look at the Montague banner and shook his head. He walked downstage, bent forward a little to clue in the audience that he was coming to the heart of his story, and said,

"...From forth the fatal loins of these two foes
A pair of star-cross'd lovers take their life;

Whose misadventure'd piteous overthrows
Doth, with their death, bury their parents' strife.
The fearful passage of their death-mark'd love
And the continuance of their parents' rage,
Which but their children's end, nought could remove,
Is now the two hours' traffic of our stage;
The which, if you with patient ears attend,
What here shall miss, our toil shall strive to mend."

Then, his story told, he bowed, and exited upstage center and through the arch.

The four boys who played the servants that start the brawl to begin the action bounced onstage as if Bill had conjured them there. In two seconds, with their insults exchanged, they were fighting, and the whole street was in an uproar. Tybalt appeared, and Benvolio, and Old Montague and Old Capulet, and then the Prince, with a few guards, to break things up and threaten everyone with the death penalty the next time they did anything like this.

And the fight came off. It was almost as realistic as the brawl I got caught in the middle of that night at the party. Maybe a little too realistic—a Montague servant went limping off at the end of the scene and he wasn't acting.

But what did that matter? The audience applauded.

One fast burst, and then they fell silent to see what would happen next.

And what happened next was magic. It was as though nobody was saying their lines, even though they were. It was guys hanging out, at high intensity, and the audience was getting sucked in. Drew was full of wicked bounce, kind of excited by the fight, and happy to tell Joey all about Tybalt, the Prince of Cats, and mocking his friend Romeo. Edmund, elegant, graceful, filling the stage with his character. And then me, finding out I was going to be married to a guy I don't know, confused, showing all of my feelings by simply twisting a small white handkerchief.

Fast forward to the balcony.

The lights dimmed as I entered. For one second, I took in the soft night, the crisp flapping of the banners *(Speak up, Miri; they're pretty loud)* and the three faint stars over my head. Then I spoke:

"Ay, me!"

Below me, Edmund turned his head toward the audience, alive with hope and lust.

"Shall I hear more, or shall I speak at this?"

And then my first famous line:

"Ah, Romeo, Romeo. Wherefore art thou Romeo?"

And we sailed together into our love.

When we were done, when Edmund had exited, and the lights went down, a wave of applause rippled across the audience, light and fresh as if the breeze had drawn it out of them along with the sound of the banners.

Nice.

My next scene was with Edmund and Phil, in Friar Lawrence's cell, where he marries us. And Phil was great. His Friar Lawrence was just like himself, a seemingly nice guy with something slightly wrong about him. When we knelt down in front of him, he moved so that the blessing hand he waved over us fell like a shadow on our faces. I saw what he was doing, and bowed my head, feeding into it. A sad, almost sinister, moment. Then it was over, and Romeo and Juliet were married and happy, and doomed. And the first act raced along to the big fight between Tybalt and Mercutio, where, just as Edmund had said that night in the bookstore, the whole play turns on what Tybalt does.

Bobby entered, smoldering with rage, and drew his sword. Drew laughed, a little nervously, and drew his. Bobby attacked, and Drew defended. He was better, but Bobby's Tybalt was empowered by a want for blood and Drew's Mercutio wasn't. Suddenly, you could see Drew's face change. He knew he was in a fight for his life. He forced Bobby back three steps, and Bobby screamed his rage. He surged back, they were nose-to-nose, then they both broke and stood panting, watching each other for the next move. Bobby would like to retreat—Mercutio's better than he realized—but he can't. Mercutio would like to laugh the thing off, but that's not going to happen and he knows it. They circle around each other, feinting with their blades.

Enter Edmund, trying to break it up. Bobby sees his chance, lunges in a perfect thrust under Edmund's arm, and Drew screams.

Drew dies, still joking, or trying to. His last line comes out of him like a sob, like a curse,

"A plague o' both your houses."

Edmund looked up at Bobby. Bobby twitched his blade.

And from somewhere out in the audience a voice wailed, "Don't do it, man!"

Taking that for his cue, Edmund attacked Bobby and cut him down. He didn't even say his speech about Mercutio's soul hovering a little way above them, waiting for one of them to join him. There wasn't time.

The audience members were really into it now. That voice in the dark had given them permission to join in. You could hear their gasps, their mutters, a few more shouts. "Cut him!" "Take him out!" And when Bobby went down, there were cheers and boos.

Then there was applause. Lots of it.

The guys in the fight scene stood there, letting it wash over them. Then Edmund did something I'd never seen anyone do onstage before. In the middle of the scene, he bowed. A long, graceful, elegant bow, the kind he'd given me when he'd thought I was Helen of Troy. He held out his arms for the rest of the actors to follow him, and they did, bowing from the waist like Americans do.

It sounds stupid, but it worked. It got the show moving again. Romeo ran off, and the scene ended.

End of act one.

The lights came up for intermission.

Bobby and Drew were hugging each other. All the guys who'd been in the scene were slapping each other on the back, and the ones who'd been watching from the wings were applauding and pumping the air with their fists.

"Oh, man," Bobby kept saying. "Oh, man."

"Yeah. But what do we do for an encore?" Drew said.

I walked over and kissed both of them. Bobby returned my kiss a little too enthusiastically. Drew gave me a fumbling peck. Then Juliet grabbed Romeo and smeared both our makeups.

"Thou art very, very hot, my lord," I said.

"Aye, but now we must recapture them," Edmund said.

And we did.

Act two scrambled along through the tight, twisty plot where everything turns on missed connections, up to the scene in the Capulets' tomb. I've taken the drug that Friar Lawrence gave me to fake death—but Romeo doesn't know I'm faking. He comes back to Verona when he hears I've died, planning to kill himself and die next to me, finds Count Paris by my grave, gets into a fight with him, kills him, takes Juliet in his arms, takes the poison, kisses me and dies. Friar Lawrence shows up, with Romeo's servant. Boy is the friar upset. But he runs off, because a bunch of constables and watchmen are coming, along with the Capulets and Montagues. Then—you know the rest—Juliet wakes up and stabs herself with Romeo's dagger.

My death scene. It was so great to die, grieving for my love, knowing I'd be back tomorrow night to do it again. That Edmund and I could go down to death like this and stand up to take bows for it. I was so sad and so happy that my tears were real. I had a hard time getting my last couple of lines out past my sobs. But I used them. I inhaled as deeply as I could, trembling so much they could see it in the back row, and plunged the dagger under my ribs. I screamed. I fell forward. I was dead.

And I lay there on top of Edmund, cherishing the gasps and "No's" and even a "Damn it to hell!" that came from the audience, our wonderful audience who had made themselves part of the play.

Almost everybody who's left alive gathers in the Capulet tomb and things get sorted out. The two families make up, the Prince promises to pardon and punish as soon as he can figure out who's guilty of what.

Lights down.

"And—we're done," Edmund whispered under me. "Get off, Miri, before I suffocate."

"As if you'd croak before you take your bows," I whispered back, and helped him up.

Around us the rest of the cast slid quietly into position for their curtain calls. Phil on the other side of Edmund. Drew on the other side of me. Bobby beside him. Mom and Dad characters on the ends, the Nurse, the Prince, and all the rest of us. Then, lights up.

Nowadays, every play gets a standing ovation. Mom says it's because tickets are so expensive that the audience are trying to convince themselves it was worth it. And we got ours. But this one was different. This one was meant. There were cheers. Some guys tore flowers out of the planters and tossed them at the stage before our security guys stopped them. (*Elizabeth Castillo's gonna have a fit,* I thought.) And best of all, I saw my mom and dad in the front row. Mom was standing and applauding and smiling and crying, and Dad was just sitting still, looking at me over the tips of his fingers like he couldn't believe what he'd seen.

I put out my hand to Mom. Then I laid it over my heart. Then I dropped into a curtsey. And when I rose, I saw that she understood what I was saying, that this night had been for her. She was clasping her hands under her face almost like she was praying.

The actors bowed. We bowed again. We bowed a third time and started to leave the stage. But they wouldn't let us. Not until we'd taken seven more bows and Gerry had flashed the lights to say "Enough already."

"I know what—let's all do this again tomorrow night!" Bobby shouted.

But the best thing was Shakespeare came over and took my hand and Edmund's and said, "I have finally seen these roles done rightly. Thank ye, brother."

"Oh, Will," Edmund said. "Thank ye."

Chapter Thirty-Three

Those hours just after an opening night are like nothing else in life. The show is over, but you don't have to go right back to reality. You can't go back. You have to have some time to decompress, to share what you've just been through with everyone else who's just been through the same thing. You have to enjoy feeling special and know that you've earned it.

Tonight, the party was at our house. And when I got there, I saw Mom and Dad had been busy. Paper lanterns had been strung in the trees, and a banner hung from the porch with big black old-fashioned letters that said: SUCH STUFF AS DREAMS ARE MADE ON. There were a couple of immense, corny Greek masks glittering silver on either side of it, and a couple of cardboard shields with the Capulet and Montague crests on them. All over the lawn were small white signs with lines from the play.

"Alas," Shakespeare said when he saw the sign. "Your noble father has quoted the wrong play. My line is, 'We are such stuff as dreams are made on, and our little life is rounded with a sleep.' 'Tis from *Midsummer Night's Dream*."

"To hell with you, Shakespeare," I laughed. "It's exactly right."

That night took off and flew and danced among the stars. Edmund and I clung to each other even while we hugged and kissed everybody else in the cast, in the world, and knew that this was only the first night of the rest of our lives.

After a while, when things were soaring past Venus, and Edmund was teaching a bunch of the cast how to dance a galliard, and I was deep in a conversation with Drew and Bobby about how we were all going to go to New York and take over Broadway next year, I turned around and saw Mom and Dad.

"Thank you, baby," Mom said and took me in her arms. "Thank you."

And I knew she was thanking me, not just for Juliet, but for all our lives together.

"Where have I been?" Dad asked as he held me. "Where have I been?"

"Doesn't matter," I said. "You're back now. Older and wiser."

"Thank you," Dad said. "For wanting me to come home."

I hugged my dad and he held me like he'd never let go again. I had never felt so good hugging him, not since I was little. I was so happy I didn't even pay attention to the screams coming from the house. Not until I heard the words, "Oh, my God, he's got a gun!"

And the sound of the shot that came rocketing out into the night.

"What in hell?" Edmund said, and ran toward the house.

I tore loose from Dad and followed him.

"Miri, don't," Mom said.

But we were all running toward the sound.

Inside, in our living room, everyone was backed against

the walls. Some of them had their cell phones out trying to reach 911.

In the center of the room was Mr. Brandstedt. He had a short black pistol in his hand, and the air was full of bitter smoke.

Crouched in one corner was Phil Hormel.

Vivian was on the floor. She had her arms around her dad's legs like an actress in some old-time melodrama. "Daddy, no..." she begged.

Mr. Brandstedt was speaking in a tight voice, speaking rapidly as if the words had been waiting years to come out and couldn't be held back any longer. I don't remember what they were. They didn't all make sense.

But the essence was clear.

Mr. Brandstedt walked stiff-legged across the floor to where Phil was cringing, trying to hold on to Maria, who was trying to pull away from him. He pointed the pistol at Phil's head, then at Maria's, then back at Phil's.

I could see Edmund crouching, getting ready to spring onto Mr. Brandstedt's back. I could see Dad trying to move up to get between Mr. Brandstedt and Phil, talking in his best shrink voice, saying he understood how much Mr. Brandstedt was hurting, how bad things must be. All this at once, and all in one second.

And then, there was a flash of light that filled the room, a clap louder than a gunshot, and Phil Hormel was gone.

Chapter Thirty-Four

Everyone screamed.

Mr. Brandstedt fired at the place where the flash had been. Then he dropped the gun.

"I—what'd I do?" he said. "Where is he? Did I kill him?"

Maria was yelling at her husband in German.

Vivian was sobbing, still on the floor.

Dad bent over and helped her stand up.

"Come and sit down," Dad said, and took her out of the way.

I could hear sirens. In a minute the cops were there and the rest of the night was ugly. Mr. Brandstedt got taken away in handcuffs.

The police questioned all of us, over and over that night. They got the same story, with minor variations, from everyone. But they couldn't, wouldn't believe Phil had simply disappeared in a noisy flash of light. No one blamed them. Half the people who'd seen it said, "I don't believe it, either."

Very early in the morning the police finally let everyone go, and left.

They'd talked to everyone but the Shakespeare brothers, who had, thankfully, managed to disappear amid all the confusion. But when Mom and Dad and Drew and Bobby and I were the only ones still sitting in the living room, they came out from wherever they'd been, leaping gracefully over the yellow tape that declared CRIME SCENE a hundred times all around our house.

"'Twas just like hiding from the game wardens in Stratford," Shakespeare said. "A most pleasant evening."

"I have never had so much fun with ye, Will," Edmund said.

"Oh, whew—you're all right then. Great," Drew said. "Well, good night, everyone. Gotta go before my mom—"

"Not so fast, Drew," Mom said. "You want to tell us what you did?"

Drew didn't answer.

"Man up, man," Bobby told him.

"We might be able to help," Dad said.

Drew sighed heavily.

"I put the Zeno program on my phone," Drew said. "So I could work on it away from home."

"I thought I had your promise not to contact Doctor Dee anymore," Mom said.

"I couldn't keep it.... I tried. I never opened that program until ten nights ago. Then I found this in my bedroom."

He reached into his pocket and pulled out a funny-looking coin. He handed it to Mom, who read its engraving aloud.

"1596."

"Read the other side," Drew said.

Mom squinted and read, "Attend me. Dr. J. Dee."

"And I ignored it," Drew said. "But...then I got this one."

He handed Dad another coin. Scratched onto one side

were the words AT ONCE, and on the other side, FOR GOD'S SAKE.

"They were appearing on my desk," Drew said. "Just coming out of nowhere. Anyway, I broke my word to you. I had to. I sent a message to Doctor Dee. He wrote back with a message for Shakespeare. It was the message he tried to give you the night you had your dream, Doctor Hoberman."

"What is my message, friend Drew?" Shakespeare said.

"It's not good. First of all, Doctor Dee told me that a man had been found wandering around Yorkshire begging for help in a dialect no one could understand. He was nearly out of his mind, but he kept saying something that sounded like 'Get me back to Omaha' over and over again. They didn't know what to do with him, so the Archbishop gave him a room in the cathedral. But he ran off and now no one knows where he is. Doctor Dee just found out about him."

The equation, I thought. *That was the man who had to balance out Edmund.*

"Then when Will came here, it meant that someone from here had to go to England," Drew went on. "Someone did. A Russian soldier named Yuri Kuznetsov. He was walking around London with a Kalashnikov rifle and a lot of attitude. The constables tried to arrest him, and he started shooting. By the time he'd used up all his ammunition, a lot of people were dead. The queen was furious and worried. What was going on? So her spies were everywhere trying to find out what was happening. Of course, Doctor Dee was the first person they thought of. Who else could do something like this? And Doctor Dee told them everything he knew. So now her majesty has demanded that both the Shakespeare brothers come home and all connection between us and England stop for all time. Otherwise, she'll execute Doctor Dee for treason. And hang Joan Hart for witchcraft."

"Our sister!" Edmund shouted.

"Monstrous," Shakespeare said. "Doctor Dee is the queen's own cousin."

"The queen has a point," Dad said. "She's a ruler—she has to protect her people. And if Russian soldiers are slipping randomly into the sixteenth century, what's next?"

Dad was being reasonable. How could he be reasonable at a time like this?

"So that's when I started working again on the program," Drew said. "Because I've never been able to send anything but words and ideas before. It's Doctor Dee who can send objects and people. He gave me some ideas on pentagrammatic geometry that I thought might work. So I added a pentagram to the program."

"So you tested it on Phil Hormel," Mom said.

"We were hanging out on the front porch," Bobby jumped in. "And we saw Vivian's dad come up the walk. And it was dark, but Drew said, 'Isn't that a pistol in his hand?' and the guy walked right past us and into the house and nobody but us even noticed the gun."

"I knew what he was going to do," Drew said. "I mean, it was obvious. And my first thought was, *'I have to save Phil.'* I turned on the app and pointed the phone and hoped it would work."

"So now Phil is running around 1597?" I said.

"Probably," Drew said.

"Hey, at least he's still alive," Bobby said.

"Unless he's not," Mom said.

"Drew. You have to contact Doctor Dee," Dad said. "There may already be another Elizabethan Englishman lost somewhere in this century."

"Right," Drew agreed, and started Achilles running after the turtle on his damned cell phone.

No, I thought. *This can't happen. Edmund can't go. There's a way*—but I couldn't think of what it was.

In a few minutes, Drew had mail.

One fellow is here, most confused, distressed and frighted. And he has good right to be, for if the Queen's minions find him, he is a dead man as I may well soon be. Doctor Jenkins, if ye love me, send the Shakespeare brothers back. I will bend my best efforts to return this hapless one to you.

Everyone was quiet.

My mind was jumping like a caught rabbit. *Edmund, Edmund, Edmund, Edmund. There's a way for us. There has to be. We belong together. Here. Now.*

Finally, Edmund spoke. "I am undone. I must go back."

"Aye, and that soon," Shakespeare said. "Damn her royal majesty to hell. But there is no choice." He looked around at all of us with his huge, beautiful eyes. "I like this place," he said sadly. "And willingly could waste my time in it."

"No," I said. "Don't leave, Edmund. Drew will figure something out. He always does." Even as I said it, I knew it was useless. What was Edmund supposed to do? Let his sister hang and Doctor Dee be tortured to death?

"I would if I could," Drew said. "Honestly."

"I know ye would, Drew. Though I know also we love the same girl. Ye are a noble heart. No better friend—"

Drew? Loves *me? What the hell? No way. We're friends.*

But it was true. I could tell by looking at him.

Edmund crossed the room and took me in his arms for

what we both knew was the last time. "I shall never marry. Farewell, my lovely spirit. My admired Miranda."

Now I knew what Juliet felt like when she woke up in the tomb and discovered Romeo's body.

"Come, brother," Shakespeare said. "Long goodbyes are saddest."

"Edmund," I whispered.

One last kiss. Then he pushed me away.

"Farewell, wondrous friends," Shakespeare said. "Look for yourselves in my folio. Mayhap we shall meet again there."

"Thanks for everything, guys," Bobby said. His voice was choking. "Break 'em."

"Are you ready?" Drew asked in a soft voice.

"Never," Edmund said. "But begin anyway. Be good to her. I know ye will."

Drew pointed his cell phone at Shakespeare and Edmund. There came the low, rumbling thrill, the flash and both men were gone.

I felt like my legs wouldn't work. Like my heart had stopped. Like my head was going to spin off. I was icy cold, and my heart was bleeding.

I looked at the empty place where Edmund had been a moment before. Then I turned to Drew.

"Drew," I said. "I never want to see you again."

Chapter Thirty-Five

That was last year. It seems like yesterday. It seems like a century ago. Or four.

But it's over. Somewhere, William Shakespeare is writing another play. Edmund is acting, or juggling in front of a pub, trying to make a living as an actor. There's no way to make contact, ever again. Drew wiped the memory on his computer and his cell phone.

Phil Hormel turned up at Drew's house later the same day that Edmund left forever. He was almost out of his mind. The police investigated, but what was there to investigate? A man had disappeared, now he was back. Phil sold his house and moved far away. Nobody's seen or heard from him since then.

Mr. Brandstedt got slapped with a weapons charge and had to do a lot of community service. He and Maria are still married.

We actually went on with the play. We had to. So many people in the cast had money in it we had to try to earn it back. So Bobby took Romeo and Vivian took Juliet and good old Bill Meisinger did Friar Lawrence and the Chorus. The show did okay.

Better than okay, I guess The Ashland apprenticeships went to Bobby and Vivian. They each got cast in small parts, and started dating after they got back from Ashland. They're the hot couple of local theater, talking about all the shows they're going to do in college. I'm good with it. I haven't done a play since *Romeo and Juliet.* I can't get interested in theater again. It hurts too much.

I've just been going through the motions. I concentrate on my grades because I don't have anything else to do. I keep to myself. When Edmund's fake birth certificate finally arrived in the mail, I didn't even tear it up. I just threw it in the trash.

Lately, I've been reading in the folio, looking for characters in the plays that might be us. In *King Lear* there's a villain named Edmund. I wonder if Shakespeare wrote it for his brother. And maybe Mom is in *The Winter's Tale* as Paulina, the noblewoman who stands up for the truth against the king. It's the kind of thing Mom would do. And maybe I'm Miranda in *The Tempest* and maybe Dad is the duke-magician who makes everything happen. There's no way to know, of course. Reading the plays is just a way to touch that amazing few weeks when I was magical and in love.

I cast a spell to make me Juliet. It worked. But I forgot that *Romeo and Juliet* is a tragedy. I got what I asked for.

Drew took me at my word. He's left me alone, and at school I don't ever look his way. But just lately I've been missing him a little. He was part of that whole crazy, magical summer. And being alone all the time is beginning to lose some of its charm.

So today, for the first time in six months or so, when school was over I waited for Drew by his car.

"Give me a lift?" I said.

He opened the door for me.

We didn't talk on the way home. But I was surprised to find how much I enjoyed being back in that silly little 2CV that could carry a basket of eggs across a plowed field and never break one. It was the first time since Edmund vanished that I'd felt any good memories from that time.

When we got to my place, we parked at the curb because one of Dad's clients was in the driveway. Dad's been getting a lot of work lately.

"Do you miss working with Doctor Dee?" I asked.

"I miss—everybody. All of it," Drew said. "Well, except for the part when I worried that time might be coming apart."

"I'm sorry I said I never wanted to see you again," I said.

"I don't blame you," Drew said. "If I had the choice, I'd never see me again, either."

I laughed. It wasn't much of a laugh, but it was my first one in months.

"You were the best friend he had, Drew," I said.

"Maybe. But I was the one who made it possible for him to go back."

I closed my eyes. "But I was the one that brought him. And that started everything else. At the end, there were no choices left."

"Not quite," Drew said. "We did have choices. But we made the choices that we had to make."

"Well," I said. "That's one definition of tragedy."

"Ha, too true, I guess," Drew said, and then we both looked across the parking lot in silence for a moment.

"I want some coffee," I said. "Do you want some?"

"Yes."

We drove to Malpaso Row and parked. We walked past

the plaza where we'd staged the play a year ago. The banners were all gone. The set had been struck. There was no sign that there'd ever been a play there, one night when a cast of actors and its audience had made one great night of theater. That's the way theater is. It leaves nothing behind, unless it changes you in some way.

I had been Juliet.

I had taken a try at being Beatrice.

Maybe now was time to be Miranda.

I took Drew's hand. It was warm and strong. It wasn't like holding Edmund's hand had been, but I liked the glow it gave me.

"I've missed you, Mercutio," I said.

"I've missed *you,*" Drew answered.

We pushed through the bookstore door. Our hands stayed locked together.

★ ★ ★ ★ ★

Historical Note

Edmund Shakespeare was born in 1580 and died in 1607. He worked as an actor in London at the same time his brother William was writing the greatest plays in the English language. He never married, but he had a daughter who died before she was two. That is all that we know about him, except for one fact. When he died, someone paid a pound to have all the bells rung from the Church of Saint Saviour on the day of his funeral. A pound was a great deal of money to spend on bells. If William Shakespeare gave the money for the bells, it may well be that he loved his brother very much.

Quotes Note

Readers may notice that Edmund spends a lot of time quoting from his brother's plays. Some readers may even notice that his quotes all come from plays that were written after 1597. This is intentional. Shakespeare had no problem with taking inspiration anywhere he could find it, and of course one of Edmund's problems with his big brother in *The Juliet Spell* is exactly this.

We've been quoting Shakespeare for four hundred years. Who was *he* quoting?

Readers of this story finally have the answer.

Acknowledgments

I wish to thank Sam Krow-Lucal for his background information on acting Shakespeare; Charles McKiethan, of Thrust, which builds the sets for theaters all over the San Francisco Bay area for information on set construction; Carol Wolf for her insights into the structure of *Romeo and Juliet;* and my wife, JoAnn, for her help with a very difficult story.